CANDLELIGHT REGENCY SPECIAL

CANDLELIGHT ROMANCES

THE
BARTERED
BRIDE

Anne Hillary

A CANDLELIGHT REGENCY SPECIAL

Published by
Dell Publishing Co., Inc.
1 Dag Hammarskjold Plaza
New York, New York 10017

ISBN: 0-440-10912-4

Printed in the United States of America

First printing—June 1979

To Mary Kay,
for all her help.

CHAPTER ONE

"I'm afraid that your father didn't leave you much besides all these debts. Anything that might have been sold to pay them off went long ago, and what they brought in was rarely used to reduce the debts your father was incurring. More likely, he used the money to finance a new gambling spree."

Mr. Bennet looked over to the person he was addressing. Robin Michael Prentice was a young man of medium height and slender build. His serious nature made him appear older than his twenty-five years. Few people would guess, from his worn appearance, that he was actually Lord Scotney, the fifth Earl of Scotney.

At the moment, he was staring out the window. It was so covered with grime and soot on the outside and dust on the inside that very little could be seen through it. It was better, however, than staring at the depressing pile of bills that seemed to be his father's total legacy to him. He fingered the frayed edge of his bottle-green coat. Actually the whole coat was badly worn. Mr. Bennet hoped that he had not planned to buy a new wardrobe with his inheritance. Robin released the coat and turned to his lawyer.

"What about Claude's affairs?" he asked.

Mr. Bennet shook his head sadly. "There's nothing much there, I'm afraid. It's a pity Claude was so like your father. . . . No disrespect intended, of course," he added, remembering suddenly that he was speaking of Robin's dead brother.

Robin smiled at Mr. Bennet's embarrassment. "For goodness sakes," he said. "Say what you think. You know very well that I couldn't abide Claude. I'm not about to pretend a feeling that was never there." Robin walked back over to his chair. "We had little in common as children because he was fourteen years older than I, but even as adults, we had no mutual interests. I had no taste for gambling after seeing what my father's gaming did to my mother."

He picked up a pile of bills from the desk in front of him and idly flipped through them.

"My father was always convinced," Robin continued, "that Claude would be the one to mend the family fortune. That's what he constantly said, until Claude came to believe it too. But it was a lot of nonsense. Claude was just as bad at cards as my father."

Mr. Bennet was studying his papers with sudden intentness and seemed strangely reluctant to meet Robin's eyes. He tugged lightly at his collar and asked if the Earl would like some tea.

Robin was not moved by this sudden burst of courtesy. "Obviously there's something else. What is it? Another debt? I don't think I'd be able to notice if another was added to this pile."

"Well, actually, it's not a debt," Mr. Bennet faltered. "Well, in a way it is . . . but different, you know. More the result of an old debt."

As Mr. Bennet became more flustered, Robin grew more apprehensive. His lawyer had not hesitated to lay out his father's debts and speak openly of them. Surely this new thing could not be worse than the thousands of pounds of debts that his father had accumulated.

"Really, it's more from Claude that you're getting this," Mr. Bennet stumbled on. "Your father really meant it for him. Of course, with Claude dying a few days before your father, you are your father's heir, no doubt about that."

"Come on, man. Out with it. Your dithering is more frightening than anything else could be." Robin was clearly getting impatient.

Mr. Bennet swallowed, then plunged ahead. "It's about Miss Tolbert."

"Who?" Robin asked.

"Did your father never mention her?" Mr. Bennet did not need to see Robin shake his head to know the answer to that. The old Earl always left unpleasant tasks to the last possible moment, in the hopes he would not have to do them.

"Mary Tolbert," Mr. Bennet said quietly, "is your betrothed." He looked up long enough to take in Robin's stunned appearance, then continued to search through his papers. He pulled one out.

"Here's the original contract between her father and yours. It was made up some time ago. I had assumed that you knew about it."

He handed Robin a piece of paper. Not that Robin was in any state to absorb the contents, but it gave Mr. Bennet more confidence to pass around legal documents.

"I think there must be some mistake," Robin finally said. "I know nothing about this woman. I never agreed to any betrothal. I couldn't afford a wife if I wanted one, and, God knows, I don't want one."

He glanced down at the paper he held. He tried reading it, hoping to find it was all a joke, but the light was so bad that he could make out very little of it. He could clearly see his father's signature at the bottom, though. Thomas Prentice always signed his name with a flourish, even on his vouchers, saying honest gambling debts were nothing to be ashamed of.

"Is this thing legal?" Robin asked after giving up his attempt to decipher its contents.

"I'm afraid it is. In fact it's about as tight as could be. It appears that Miss Tolbert or her father wanted to be sure that there were no loopholes to release you from it."

Robin sighed and pushed the contract back across the desk. "Maybe you had better begin at the beginning and tell me everything you know about this"—he was at a loss for a word—"arrangement."

"Well," Mr. Bennet began, "it started about ten years ago. Soon after you lost, er . . . your father lost, that country house near Warwick."

Robin nodded, remembering the house they had all loved and had to leave when it was sold to pay their father's debts. Mr. Bennet walked across the room as he continued.

"The house was sold, but there were still more debts. We didn't get a good price for the house because everyone knew it had to be disposed of quickly. There was no time to hold out for a better price."

Mr. Bennet opened a dusty cabinet in the corner and pulled out a sparkling decanter of claret and two equally shining glasses. He ruthlessly shoved papers away from the edge of his desk, put the glasses down, and poured the wine. He handed a glass to Robin.

"There wasn't much else that could be sold. You had only Scotney Park and the townhouse in London. Both of those were entailed, but they wouldn't have brought in much anyway. The house in London isn't in a popular neighborhood, and Scotney Park was in such bad repair." He looked up briefly. "I hope I haven't offended."

Robin waved off the insults to his homes. Mr. Bennet was right. They would have brought in very little.

"Well, your father was going to break up the sets of rubies and diamonds that your mother had, but he couldn't find them. She was forever hiding things she thought he'd sell. I can't blame her, actually. Your father had long since gone through her settlement. The only thing that she could save for herself, and you and Claude, was what she managed to hide from him. That's how she paid the household expenses. So your father couldn't find the jewels and was getting desperate to pay off his creditors. It seems everyone was hounding him for money. He reached the point where he was talking of fleeing the country, when Mr. Tolbert came to see me. He had heard of the Earl's problems and was willing to help him out. For a price. He would pay off the debts if the Earl would agree to Claude becoming betrothed to Tolbert's eldest daughter."

Robin looked up, ready to pounce on Mr. Bennet's last sentence, but was stopped by the lawyer's upraised hand. Mr. Bennet paused long enough to refill their glasses.

"Your father jumped at the chance. He was an honorable man, in his own way, and didn't want to skip out on his debts. Besides, he always felt he would win everything back. He and Claude went out to Crofton Grange, where the Tolberts live, and met the girl. Apparently, all went well, because soon they were back here, ready to draw up the contract.

"The thing is," Mr. Bennet said, "they never mentioned Claude by name. He is always referred to in the contract as your father's heir. Because Claude died a few days before your father, you are your father's heir, and the contract is as binding on you as it would have been on Claude, had he lived."

The hope that had been growing in Robin's eyes died at these words. He refilled his glass. After a few sips, he looked at Mr. Bennet.

"Why didn't they ever mention Claude by name?" he asked. "It seems a silly way to write a contract."

Mr. Bennet wondered if the claret was stronger than he remembered. Surely the reason was obvious. "I don't think," he said, choosing his words carefully, "that Claude was the important part of the document."

Robin still looked confused.

"To be blunt, my lord, it was only the title that was of importance to the Tolberts, not who actually was the possessor of it. It wasn't important whether Miss Tolbert married Claude or you, as long as she married the title. That's why it had to be the heir."

"Sounds like a lovely wife that my father chose for me," Robin said. He waited while Mr. Bennet refilled the glasses from a new bottle. Then he picked his up and walked over to the window. It had started to rain, but instead of washing some of the dirt off the pane, it seemed to solidify it. The room got even darker. Mr. Bennet's oil lamp was smoking badly, and there was a perpetual smell of cigars in the air.

Mr. Bennet seemed to belong in the room. He, too, was colorless and drab. He was short and thin, with wisps of gray hair covering his almost bald head. His glasses slid down his nose as he spoke, and he peered out over them when he wanted to make a point. He was thoroughly knowledgeable in his field, but he lacked the necessary aggression to be a real success in it.

"How did my father ever happen to choose you to handle his business affairs?" Robin asked.

Normally such a question might have hurt Mr. Bennet, but after half a bottle of wine, he did not see anything strange or insulting about it.

"We were in school together, you know. Oxford. Not in the same set, of course. My uncle was putting me through, and I really had to apply myself. Didn't have much time to play.

"Your father used to gamble quite a bit, even then. He didn't have much money, but the stakes weren't very high. Well, one night he got into a place that was way out of his league and lost heavily. He was in debt with all of his friends because he had already lost that quarter's allowance. One of his friends, who was also my cousin, brought him to me, hoping I would lend him some, or, more likely, that I would borrow from my uncle to help Thomas. I had almost no money of my own, and I wasn't about to jeopardize my education by tricking my uncle into paying the gambling debts of someone I didn't even know. But I promised to help, if I could." He stopped speaking long enough to take a long drink of his wine.

"In one of my classes, we had been studying obscure local laws and the reasons behind them. A few days after your father came to see me, I discovered that the gambling house was in a building that had originally been part of a church, and its present use was forbidden by one of these local laws. The authorities were notified, and the place was closed down. They never had a chance to collect from your father. That convinced him that I had a resourcefulness that could pull him out of any difficulty. So, when he came into his inheritance and could choose his own lawyer, he picked me. Unfortunately, I was never able to help him quite like that again, but then neither was I paid much for my services, so I suppose he felt we were even."

Robin looked at him. "You shouldn't have gotten mixed up with him. You should have stuck to people who were willing to pay their fees."

Mr. Bennet shrugged. "My other clients do. Maybe that's why I felt I could cling to my one titled one."

The reference to his title brought Robin back to the problem at hand. "There must be some way to get out of this contract. Why didn't Claude marry her long ago?"

"I'm not sure of all the details. I had actually forgotten about it until I was going through your father's papers. I know that one of the things that held it up was raising the settlement."

Robin groaned. "So, besides getting a wife I don't want, I've got to scrape together enough money to buy her? Do you think I could just go to debtor's prison and forget all about it?"

"The settlement is no problem," Mr. Bennet reassured him. "It's all in the contract. Part of the income from the farms at Scotney Park has been put into a fund for the past ten years. There's not a great deal there, because the farms have needed much repair, but it is slightly over the agreed-on figure of five thousand pounds. Of course, it's just a token figure. Miss Tolbert received most of her grandmother's estate and is wealthy in her own right. So you see, once you are married you will be able to pay these other debts."

"That is a great consolation," Robin said, pouring himself more wine. "I think, however, I'd rather have my debts." He took a long drink. "Here, at last, Mr. Bennet, is your chance to help me with your great resourcefulness heretofore saved exclusively for my father." Robin continued, "You must find a way to break this contract and set me free to live happily, once more, amid my debts."

Mr. Bennet thought for a moment. "What you could do," he suggested, "is pay back the original debt."

"That's just what I'll do!" Robin shouted. He jumped up, finished the wine in his glass, and asked, "How much was it?"

Mr. Bennet searched through the pile of papers until he found what he wanted.

"Sixty-four thousand pounds," he said.

Robin turned pale and barely made the chair before he sat down. The effects of the wine had rapidly worn off both of them.

"I couldn't raise even ten thousand pounds if

my life depended on it. There's no way that I could get that much money, not legally anyway."

Visions of the fifth Earl of Scotney, with a mask covering his face, holding loaded pistols on rich travelers came into Mr. Bennet's head.

"I doubt that he'd take it back anyway," he said, hoping to dispel the vision. "He was awfully set on having his daughter marry well."

"You're probably right. He'd never give up a live, titled pigeon, when he had one trapped."

Robin spoke so bitterly that Mr. Bennet was shocked. He had always liked Robin, because he was easy to understand. He hadn't really liked Thomas or Claude; he had been more in awe of them. They lived in a way that was so unrestricted that Mr. Bennet couldn't help but envy them slightly. It wasn't fair, though, for Robin to have to pay for their irresponsibility. Maybe the way they lived wasn't to be envied after all.

"I've written to Mr. Tolbert," Mr. Bennet said. "I felt he should be notified of Claude's and your father's deaths. He is very anxious to have the wedding take place soon. He feels there has been too much delay as it is. Asks that you come down at your convenience."

Robin said nothing but reached out for the letter his lawyer had in his hand. He put it in his pocket and picked up his hat and gloves.

"I guess I had best go meet my loving bride," he said. He nodded to Mr. Bennet and went down the stairs and out into the rain.

* * *

After he left Mr. Bennet's office, Robin made the rounds of his clubs, looking for his friends. (In spite of all his father's debts and gambling losses, he insisted that both of his sons belong to the best clubs in London.) It was at White's that he eventually ran down some of his friends.

A few of them had been at Oxford together; the rest had met on the Continent. After Waterloo, they drifted back to London. In the year since their return, they had tried to avoid any permanent ties. Lately, though, Tom Wentworth was seen less with them and more in the company of a rather plump little brunette who had, besides bright blue eyes and appealing dimples, a strange liking for the climate of Northumberland, where Tom's estate just happened to be located. Two others, Ralph Crinnam and Vernon Tatterly, were talking of emigrating to America to start a shipping business. They were both younger sons and had no financial responsibilities in England. The carefree air that had characterized previous gatherings of the old friends was fading. However reluctant they were, they all seemed to be heading toward some settling of their futures.

On this evening, Robin found only Sir Matthew Trilby, a friend from Oxford, and Tom Wentworth, engaged in a game of faro at White's. The game broke up soon after Robin's arrival because Tom was anxious to be off. He had plans for dinner and an evening at Vauxhall Gardens. Since his entire conversation dealt with boat rides, walks through the gardens, and a certain someone's blue eyes, no one tried very hard to detain him. Once he had taken his leave, Robin and Trilby breathed sighs of relief.

"Have to say, I won't be sorry to see old Tom get leg shackled," Sir Matthew said. "Hope his conversation improves when he does. 'Course, if he goes up to his estate, we won't be hearing much from him anyway. Every time he talks, I'm afraid he's going to spout verse." He shuddered visibly. "Do me a favor, old boy?" he asked of Robin. "If I ever get in such a depressing condition, shoot me. Or push me in the river. It'd be better in the end. I'd hate to be reduced to sending flowers and penning verse."

Robin laughed at him. "I seem to remember a fragile looking blonde named Arabella who received a great many yellow roses from you last year. Maybe even a poem or two."

Trilby had the grace to look embarrassed. "Well, of course. She was all the rage last year. You wouldn't have me out of fashion, would you? Besides, I was lost in the crowds around her. Rather glad, too. She was a frightening woman. Too tall. I didn't write the verses, though. Diane wrote them for me. She was going through a poem writing phase. Paid her a penny a poem."

Robin was laughing quite loudly, to the disapproval of some of the older members, who were frowning at them from across the room. "Damn, that's a good one," he said, wiping his eyes. "I just wish Arabella had known you were paying your little sister to write verse for you. She put it all about town that you were wild for her. Constantly making her offers. I thought you were going to desert us for her."

"Lord, help me. I never made her an offer. Was never alone with her. The truth was, my mother was after me to settle down. Kept pushing Rose Tremaine at me."

"Was she the skinny one with spots?" Robin asked.

"Goodness, no. Rose was the one with all the teeth. Looked like a horse. She was always on one, too. I always feared that she'd want to be married on horseback."

"Why was your mother so keen on her? I wouldn't think you two would suit," Robin commented, for Trilby had been known throughout their regiment as the only cavalry officer who would rather walk.

"My mother and hers were old friends. Shared secrets in the schoolroom, or some such thing. I can't bear to listen when my mother gets started on the tales of her youth. Anyway, Arabella was quite handy. I followed her all over, but I was quite safe in the crowd. Told my mother I was following the dictates of my heart. What I didn't say was that my heart was dictating to remain free."

The disapproving glares from across the room could no longer be ignored, so Robin and Trilby decided to leave before they were thrown out of the club.

It was still raining when they got outside, and Trilby insisted that they hire a hack.

"You wouldn't want to be responsible for the ruin of this fine coat, would you?" he asked Robin.

Robin looked at his friend. Trilby was a very large man and he chose to wear very bright clothes, which only accentuated his size. This evening he was wearing a well-made gray coat, which was surprisingly subdued for him. Underneath it, however, was a waistcoat of magenta brocade. The little of it that Robin could see was enough to convince him that Trilby had really outdone himself when he chose it.

"No," laughed Robin, "I wouldn't want anything to happen to your coat. Right now, it's all that's protecting me from that waistcoat."

Trilby looked down at the offending garment. "Isn't it a beauty?" he asked.

Robin was saved from having to answer by the appearance of a hackney on the road near the club. They flagged him down and directed him to Upper Wimpole Street, where the Earl's house was located.

"Can't see why you have a house in this neighborhood," said Trilby. "You ought to get rid of it and find yourself a more fashionable spot."

Robin nodded absently, for he was trying to indicate to the jarvey which house was his. They finally pulled up to a depressingly dark entryway. The young men alighted and paid off the hack.

The door was opened, after a few minutes' wait,

by a middle-aged man named Sourly, who looked exactly as his name implied. He took their hats, gloves, and topcoats and settled them in a dark room toward the back of the house. It was this room that the fourth Earl had called his library, for it held his entire collection of books. There were about one hundred altogether—all the ones that were in such poor condition that they could not be sold to the used-book dealers.

The rest of the room was dominated by a massive fireplace. It actually had some fine carvings holding up the mantel, but they were so covered with soot and dust that they were no longer distinguishable. In spite of the gloominess of the room, there was a comfortable feeling in it, but it could have been created by the brandy that was served, or the warm fire in the grate.

Robin and Trilby sat down near the fire in a more cheerful frame of mind than Robin thought possible earlier in the day. Sourly brought glasses and a decanter, and Robin ordered their dinner to be prepared. They were well through their second glass by the time the butler returned to announce that their meal was ready.

They proceeded through a passable meal and two bottles of wine. One thing the old Earl had liked was his wine. He had an excellent, if small, wine cellar. After dinner they returned to the library, where Sourly had refilled the brandy decanter. They settled down near the fire. Trilby was just about asleep when Robin looked up.

"Did your mother buy the story about Arabella and forget about horsy Rose?"

Trilby stared at Robin for a minute, until the question finally penetrated. "Oh, yes. She bought it, all right. She began making plans for my marriage to Arabella, though. 'Course, when she got herself engaged to Markham, my mother was a bit upset. Kept talking about my wife marrying someone else. Tried again with Rose, but I pleaded a broken heart, and I didn't recover until Rose was safely married."

Robin stared into the fire. A log cracked and fell with a shower of sparks.

"Trilby, I think you're just the man I need to get me out of a fix." He took a long drink. "Ever hear of the Tolberts?"

Sir Matthew took on a pensive look, but in reality, he was having trouble concentrating. "Don't think so. Are they new in town?"

"I," said Robin, "am to marry the eldest Miss Tolbert, by the kind design of my benevolent parent."

"When'd you meet her?" Trilby asked. "You never mentioned it before. Damn, if I'm not hurt. Damn if I don't leave." He made no move toward the door, though. He merely went to refill his glass.

"Couldn't tell anybody because I didn't know until today. Seems my father got badly dipped about ten years ago, and Tolbert offered to pay his debts if his heir would marry Tolbert's eldest daughter. Father agreed, and the papers were signed, all very tight. Not a loophole, according to Bennet. Although someone with your resourcefulness and lack of ethics should be able to do better."

"She must have been a real antidote even then if her father had to buy her a husband. She's had ten years since then. Do you suppose she's shaped up? How old is she?"

"I don't know, exactly." Robin tried to remember if Mr. Bennet had mentioned her age. "Don't think it was referred to. Claude was supposed to be the groom, though, so I'd imagine that she was closer to his age. I wish he had married her. I'd much rather have her as Claude's widow than my wife."

Trilby looked up from the brandy he'd been studying. "Maybe Claude picked an early death rather than wed his chosen goddess. Had he seen her? Maybe she was just too awful, even for Claude's strong palate."

Robin shook his head soberly, but a grin could be seen in his eyes. "Claude was not exactly the soul of honor. He would have eloped with someone else or fled the country if he was really desperate to avoid her. Besides, he wouldn't have minded all her money. I doubt that he killed himself. Might be an idea for me, though. I shall leave you everything I possess, including Sourly."

"Ah, my boy," said Trilby, "that is just the incentive I needed to find you a solution. It's really very simple. She must choose herself another husband."

"Shall I tell her, or will you?" Robin asked.

"Silence, you disbeliever," Trilby said, handing

his empty glass to Robin to refill. "You have to work for the results of my wisdom."

When Robin had returned a full glass to Trilby, he was ready to continue. "You, my good friend, are not the greatest charmer of the fair set that I have ever known. In fact, I might go so far as to say you haven't the faintest notion how to charm the lady of your dreams into fulfilling them." He waved aside Robin's pained expression. "Some other day, I will take you under my wing for expert guidance, but in this instance it is to your advantage to be yet untutored."

Trilby took a long drink, then went on. "Who would you say, to your inexpert eye, has the touch of greatness when it comes to charming the ladies? The respectable ones, that is."

Robin thought for a moment. "Excluding you, of course, I'd say Fulton, or Smithington, or Merriot."

"Sir Julian Merriot. Precisely who I had in mind. A mere baronet, of course. I say 'mere' because, unlike some other baronet present here that I could name, he lacks the necessary funds to maintain himself in any sort of style at all. He is a fortune hunter, to be blunt. A charming, middle-aged fortune hunter. Just what we need."

Trilby was so involved in his discourse that he did not notice Robin's confused look or his empty glass. Robin refilled again and begged him to continue his enlightening lecture.

He ignored Robin's sarcasm and said plainly, "We must tell Merriot that there is a rather plain heiress in Crofton who is looking for a husband, and persuade him to use all his charm on her. He can't really expect to get any of the young things he's been angling after. If we lead him to believe he has a real chance with her, he might use the right technique to sweep a certain lady right off her feet and down the aisle with him, instead of you."

Robin had lost his look of disbelief. "It sounds so simple. Do you really think it would work?"

"Certainly," said Trilby. "Merriot is desperate to get married. I've heard that his creditors are putting a lot of pressure on him. If he can marry her, his troubles are over and so are yours. Her father can't complain if you are willing to go through with it but the bride wants somebody else, can he?"

Robin felt that the logic in that argument was a little strained, but it did seem to make sense. "What if the father is still set on me as the groom?" There was still that lurking fear.

"Well, then we would make you into a despicable cad, but I don't think we would get to that point. If you give Merriot a few days' head start, he ought to be doing well by the time that you appear. You'll definitely lose by comparison."

That seemed like a remark to argue over, but because Robin did want to lose by comparison, he let it go by.

"Just act rude and obnoxious," advised Trilby. "Ask the price of everything. That should hasten your defeat."

They drifted from that topic to a discussion of an upcoming cockfight not too far from Crofton and the hope that Robin would be able to get away long enough to meet some of their mutual friends there. When the brandy was gone and the fire burning low, Trilby left, promising to meet Robin the next day so they could look for Sir Julian Merriot.

As Trilby walked toward his home, he wondered how he could really help Robin. The idea that he had come up with earlier did not seem all that foolproof to him. What he felt Robin really needed was a plan that would make Mr. Tolbert positively refuse to let his daughter marry him.

He passed through an area lit from the open door of a tavern. A figure ran at him.

"A penny, sir?" a soft voice asked him. "A penny for me and my baby?"

Trilby saw a young serving girl before him. She was very young and attractive, but dressed shabbily. Held tight in her arms was a very small, sickly baby. He gave her a few coins from his pocket and hurried on his way. It was a common enough sight: a serving girl ravished, then thrown out when it was discovered that she was pregnant, but it never failed to depress him. How some men could be so despicable . . . Suddenly Trilby knew he had found the answer to Robin's dilemma.

CHAPTER TWO

Although it was warm and sunny, Robin found the ride out of London depressing. Each step the horse took was bringing him closer to Crofton, and to Miss Tolbert.

He remembered the interview with Merriot, though, and that did bring a smile to his face. He and Trilby had had a great deal of trouble finding him. After calling at his rooms unsuccessfully several times, Robin felt that they should just give up, and Trilby was trying to think of somebody else who would fit in his plan. Then they spotted him in the street ahead of them. They followed him home and demanded to be let in to see him. When they finally were admitted, Sir Julian was very apologetic.

"Sorry about all that," he told them. "My man thought you might be dunning me. Not that anybody is, mind you," he added hastily. "But there always is a first time."

Neither Robin nor Trilby quite believed his claim that no one was hounding him for the payment of bills, but they said nothing as they sat down. Sir Julian offered them some wine.

"Heard you were thinking of settling down," Trilby commented as he sipped his wine.

"Thinking of it, yes," Merriot said. "But I haven't done anything about it yet." He was not about to admit to them that he had proposed to four young girls in the past week and had been turned down by all of them.

"Shouldn't be too hard for you," Robin said. "You seem to have a way with the ladies."

"Yes, well unfortunately," Sir Julian said, "a few of their fathers take my lack of fortune in a rather bad spirit. Not that the ladies themselves ever doubt my sincerity. I pride myself on my ability to charm any lady I choose. Even the hard, dried-up spinsters. I just study them for a while, find their weaknesses, and worm my way into their good graces with my good looks and outrageous flattery. You know, it always amazes me how the ugliest, most uninteresting woman will believe it when I tell her how lovely she is."

"You certainly seem to be progressing well with a few young ladies I've seen you escorting about town," Robin said. "Are you going to try for one of those?"

Julian hesitated, not wanting to admit that he had, and had been rejected. "Actually, I prefer the older ones," he said, "the ones that don't have fathers hovering over them, making their decisions for them."

"There aren't too many older ones in town now," Trilby said.

A bell rang in the distance, and Julian sat quite still, listening. Voices could be heard arguing after Merriot's man had opened the door. A few minutes later, the door was firmly shut, and the footsteps died away. Julian relaxed.

"I think I may have to go out of town for a while," he said, in answer to Trilby's comment, "on business, you know."

Both Trilby and Robin nodded, not really knowing what to say. Robin was anxious to get to the topic that had brought them there, but he tried to be patient. Trilby had said that he would handle it when he thought the time was right.

"It's funny the number of people who are thinking of getting married these days," Trilby said.

"Oh?" said Julian, looking at the two of them. "Who are the lucky ladies?"

"Not either of us," Robin said hastily. "You know, just rumors about other people."

"Why, we've even heard of some woman in Crofton who's looking around for a husband," Trilby said.

"Crofton?" asked Julian. "I don't think I've even heard of that town."

"She's got a lot of money," Robin threw in, "so she's bound to have a number of suitors to choose from."

"Oh, *that* Crofton," Julian said. "I remember the town quite well. North of London, I believe?"

"No, south of it. On the road to Brighton," inserted Trilby. "Maybe you know the family. Name of Tolbert."

Julian shook his head slowly. "No, I don't think I've ever had the pleasure, but as it happens, I was planning on going that way in a few days. Perhaps I might run into them."

"Wouldn't that be a coincidence," said Trilby, giving Robin a knowing look. "We'd better be going, don't you think, Robin?"

Robin agreed rather reluctantly. Once they were outside, he turned to his friend.

"Why did you want to leave just then? We were starting to tell him about Miss Tolbert. Are you planning to go back there again to tell him more?"

Trilby laughed. "I don't think we'd catch him unless we went right back now. I'm sure he is already planning an immediate trip to Crofton to seek out the mysterious Miss Tolbert."

"I hope you're right," Robin said gloomily.

A few days later, Robin took his leave of Trilby. He was going to visit Scotney Park briefly and then go to Crofton to meet the Tolberts. Unfortunately the road to his estate first went through Crofton, so he wasn't proceeding too eagerly. He wasn't known in the area, so he didn't think it would matter if he went through the town.

As he rode along, Robin began to think about his estate. He wondered what condition it was in. Although it had been his home when he was growing up, it was years since he had been there last. He was looking forward to living there. The house was probably in need of repair, and the farms had not produced well in the last few years, but it was a good kind of life. He could work hard at it and make it productive once more. He was getting tired of the aimless drifting that he had been doing in the past year. And he certainly had not wanted to make a career in the army. The only problem he could see in his immediate future was this woman whom his father had picked out for him.

The thought of settling down to a quiet life in the country with a wife was appealing to him, but not with a woman he didn't even know. He wanted to marry someone who would share his dreams and be content to live quietly at the park until his finances were in better condition.

He wanted to be friends with his wife. He wanted to have someone he could talk to, someone he had something in common with. Life in the country was considerably different from that in the city. In town, you might not see your wife for days if she liked to socialize a great deal. Of course, if you didn't care too much for her, that was a blessing. On the other hand, on an estate you would be together much of the time. Any parties that you might attend were small and quiet. He smiled as he imagined the shocked faces of some of the older people in the area if he and his wife never appeared together at the neighborhood functions. He hoped that he would have at least a few things in common with Miss Tolbert. To be restricted to the park with someone he couldn't even talk to was something he did not want to contemplate.

He tried to console himself with the thought of the bills her money would pay, but along with the money, he would be getting a wife who saw him only as a title, whereas he saw her as a way out of debt.

Robin was slightly delayed by a storm, but he was passing through Crofton by the middle of the afternoon. It was a larger town than he had expected and seemed very busy, as the London-to-Brighton stage had just passed through. In all the confusion, no one noticed him, and he saw no one he knew.

He was getting hungry and thirsty but was loathe to prolong his stay in town. He decided to find an inn along the road once he was safely past Crofton. With the thought of a cool glass of ale in mind, he pushed farther along.

Once Robin decided that it would be safe to stop, there were no inns in sight. He traveled about a mile down the road, cursing his caution, when he spied a creek running not too far from the road. He turned his horse toward it, thinking that a cool drink of water was not quite what he had wanted, but it would help stave off thirst.

Along the edge of the creek grew a great many bramble bushes, and a little way in from the road, Robin saw the remains of a wall that was in a sad state of disrepair. He hoped he might squeeze between the bushes and the wall, but when he got near he saw that it would be impossible. The bushes were so close to the wall that he couldn't get through without having his clothes torn and his face and hands badly scratched.

He decided to jump the wall and look for a better place. His horse took it quite easily, but as he touched down, Robin heard a scream very close at hand. Thinking he was about to land on someone, he pulled his horse up short so that it stumbled, and Robin was almost thrown. He regained his balance and looked around, not in the best of moods. He forgot his anger when he saw a young girl, obviously the screamer, very close by. Her riding habit and her hair were tangled in the bushes. He dismounted quickly.

The thorny bushes almost completely surrounded the small figure. Her hair was almost black and it made her face seem even whiter. Her eyes were dark blue, accented by the blue of her riding habit. Her face was smeared with mud and her hands were scratched from the thorns.

"My horse didn't hurt you, did he?" Robin thought she looked very pale.

"No, I was startled, that's all. Nobody ever comes this way. After my horse ran off, I hoped a groom would come looking for me, but it's been ages and there's been no sign of anyone. I was just trying to get myself out of this mess when your horse came sailing over." She kept pulling at her skirt as she spoke, trying to free it from the thorns, but was only succeeding in tearing the fabric.

"Here, let me help," Robin offered. "No, don't pull. Maybe I'd better start on your hair first."

He reached over to try to free it, but suddenly he was reluctant to touch it. He had never seen such beautiful hair. It was black, and the sunshine gave it streaks of blue. It was long and thick and curled around the branches as though it had grown there.

"Is something wrong?" she asked.

Robin jumped. "No," he said. "I was just trying to decide where it would be best to begin."

He touched the hair nearest him. It felt cool and soft to his touch. It was also firmly entwined around the branch. Try as he might, he couldn't seem to free much of it. He knew that he was hurting her, even though she said nothing, and it made him fumble even more. Finally he had to admit that he couldn't get it free.

"Is it that bad?" she asked, turning to face him. He knew that he had caused the tears in her eyes, and he felt very ineffective. Maybe, he thought, it's just as well I'm marrying someone who wants only my title. I'd be of no use to anyone who really needed me. He remembered Trilby's remark that he was no charmer, and he had to agree.

"Maybe you could just break off some of the branches and I could work on it at home," she suggested.

"Oh, good idea," Robin said, glad to be given something that he could do. But it wasn't as easy as it sounded to break the branches. It took much twisting and bending before she was free from the

37

rest of the bush. Even then, there were still many twigs in her hair.

Next, Robin set to work on her skirt. This was a much easier task, although he went slowly so as not to ruin the fabric.

"I'll be careful not to tear it," he told her, hoping to alleviate any doubts she had as to his competence.

"Oh, it doesn't really matter," she said. "It's already awfully worn." That was true. It had originally been a deep blue velvet, but there were many places where the velvet had worn down. As a result, it had a definitely seedy look to it.

"Nonsense," said Robin, who could see for himself that it was in poor condition. "It still has a lot of wear in it." The poor kid probably couldn't afford to get a new one, he thought. Who would let his daughter appear in such a shabby outfit if he could afford to buy her a new one?

The girl turned to smile at Robin, which so disconcerted him that he cut himself on a thorn. She decided not to tell him that she had three newer habits at home. It was only because she was such a terrible rider and could never seem to stay on a horse, that they wore out so fast. She noticed that the cuffs of his coat were threadbare and that his shirt was definitely not of the best linen, and thought perhaps genteel poverty might be the best approach.

"How did you happen to get into these bushes?" Robin was trying to divert her attention from his slow progress.

She thought for a moment. In an age when it was quite the thing for a girl to be an excellent rider, she was hesitant to admit that she couldn't take a very low wall.

"It was my horse, you see," she began. "She's not a good jumper. I've been trying to train her, but I'm afraid she just doesn't have the heart for it."

"Where'd she run off to?" Robin asked.

"She went home, through that field," she said, pointing across an adjacent field.

Robin looked the way she had indicated. He could see, stretched across the meadow, a fence that was taller than the wall behind them. As far as he could tell, the fence ran the entire length of the field. He smiled to himself as he returned to his task.

"She must have opened the gate for herself," he teased.

She looked at the meadow again and realized what he meant. "No," she admitted sadly. "She can't open gates. It was really my fault. I fell because I can't jump. I can't make myself take even this wall, so I keep coming back here to try. This is the lowest thing around, but I can't even get over that. My father is quite in despair. He feels I have no talents."

"What?" Robin laughed. "Can't you paint watercolors and play the pianoforte? I thought those were the required skills for a young lady."

"No," she said. "I can't ride well. When I was taught how to paint, I spilled my watercolors all over the other girls having lessons with me and was asked not to return. I can play a little music, but no one will stay to listen to it. My only talent is to empty out a drawing room faster than anyone else." She smiled at him.

Robin got the last of her skirt free from the thorns and helped her away from the bushes.

"What were you doing so far from the road?" she asked him. "Surely you couldn't see me all the way over there."

"No," Robin admitted, "I was trying to find a place where I could get close to the creek to get a drink. The bushes all grow so close along here, and I thought that I might find a better spot away from the road."

"Well, it was lucky for me you did. When I saw it was getting cloudy again I thought for sure I was going to be drenched before any help came. Thank you very much for your aid. I'm quite sure I would have been in a sorry state if I had had to rescue myself." She looked down at the scratches on her hands, the mud and leaves on her skirt, and felt the branches in her hair.

"Well," she laughed. "I may already be in a sorry state, but at least I'm not soaked by the rain. Come down this way and I'll show you a good spot to get a drink." She led the way along the bushes, until they came to a path that led down to the creek.

"This is used by the horses to cross the creek, but once you get down to the creek bed, you can go up it a ways until you find a good spot to drink from."

She held the reins of Robin's horse as Robin went down the path. After he was out of sight, she led the horse down to the creek so he could drink also.

It was obvious when Robin came back that he had done more than just taken a drink. He had cleaned the mud off his hands and had straightened his neckcloth and hair. He led the horse back for her but seemed reluctant to leave.

"Is there an inn nearby where I might get something to eat?" he asked.

"There are many good ones in Crofton, which isn't much farther. My brother says that the Red Dragon stocks a fine cellar."

Robin was a little embarrassed. "I've just come through there. I was looking for something a little quieter."

She looked at him in surprise. "Well, there aren't any more inns along this road for several miles. It would take you until evening to reach them."

Robin must have looked as disappointed as his stomach felt, because she told him to wait and ran back to where she had fallen.

"There's not much here," she said, holding out a small bag, "but you're welcome to it." She pulled out an apple, some bread spread with jam, and two pastries wrapped in a white napkin. "I had better start back before it begins to rain." She handed him the bag. "Thank you again."

Then she turned and ran along a path that followed the creek bed. Soon she was out of sight behind some trees.

Robin looked at the bag he was holding. The

pastries smelled good. He suddenly felt quite hungry, but, considering the look of the sky, he decided to find some shelter first. He led his horse over a crumbled section of the wall and back to the road. A short way down it, there was a thick grove of trees that would provide some protection.

Once safely under them, Robin tied his horse to a low branch and began to eat. As delicious as the food may have been, he ate without really tasting it. He could still feel soft black hair curling around his hand and see a smile that lit up a mud-smeared face. It was only then that Robin realized that he didn't know her name.

Despite a desire to meander along the creek, Kitty knew that she had better hurry home. If she was really lucky, she would make it before her father returned home from town and before it started to rain. She made it up to her room unnoticed. The house was very quiet, which probably meant that her father had not arrived yet. That gave her a little more time to make repairs. She pulled off her riding habit and left it in a pile on the floor. After washing the mud off her arms and legs, she put on a faded blue wrapper and began on her hair.

As soon as Kitty tried to untangle her hair, she knew it was much worse than she had thought. After a few minutes' struggle, she decided to cut the branches out. She found a pair of scissors and began to cut as carefully as she could. About halfway through, while she was struggling with the back, she heard the door open. The scissors were grabbed from her hand.

"What are you doing, child?"

Kitty turned and, to her relief, saw it was Maggie. She had been Kitty's mother's maid and had looked after the children since their mother had died. She turned Kitty around and inspected the mess her hair was in.

"How do you do these things?" she asked. "I sometimes think you shouldn't be allowed out on your own. Be a good thing once you're married and having babies. You'll be too busy to be getting yourself into trouble like this."

Maggie picked up the scissors and began to cut where Kitty had left off. With considerable difficulty, Kitty refrained from commenting on her upcoming marriage. Everyone in the house knew what she thought of it, so it seemed a waste of time to begin the argument all over again.

"Did all that come from me?" Kitty asked, looking at the hair on the floor when Maggie finished.

"It's not that short, honey," Maggie told her. "It don't look bad at all. It's still plenty long to put up, but maybe it won't come down so easy now that it's not so heavy.

"You'd better get dressed for dinner," Maggie told her after she cleaned up the hair. "I'll be back real soon to help you. You don't want to be late tonight. Your father has a surprise for you."

There was only one subject that would put that sparkle into Maggie's eyes, and Kitty did not want to hear about it. She did think it would be best, though, not to be late in getting downstairs if she hoped to remain inconspicuous.

Maggie was surprised when she returned a little later to find Kitty had finished arranging her hair and was choosing a dress. She had pulled her hair away from her face and let it fall into soft ringlets down her back. Because Kitty's hair curled naturally, it was an easy style to arrange, and it wasn't too obvious that her hair was shorter.

Maggie helped her into a rose-colored dress that her father had always favored. Its tight bodice and gently draped skirt enhanced Kitty's figure and made her appear taller. Maggie fastened a locket around Kitty's neck and draped a paisley shawl over her arms. Kitty took a last glance at herself in the mirror and went down to meet her family for dinner.

When Kitty entered the drawing room, the only other occupant was her brother Willy. He was a year younger than Kitty, but a full head taller, and thought he was years wiser.

Tonight he was engrossed in a deck of playing cards.

"Oh, Kitty," he said. "I've been looking for you all day. I wanted to show you a trick that Barny taught me."

Barny was one of Willy's good friends whom he had thought best never to introduce to the family. Kitty had seen him from a distance on a few occasions and had never desired closer acquaintance.

Willy was setting up a strange arrangement of

cards on a small table near the windows when they heard voices in the hall.

"Blast!" whispered Willy. He grabbed the cards and managed to stuff them behind the pillows of a nearby chair before the door opened.

Their father who did not approve of Barny or his card tricks and their sister Alicia came in. Although Alicia was only sixteen, she often looked, and acted, older than Kitty. She took more time with her appearance and wanted to experience the social life of London more than anything else. She spent her time equally divided between reading the social column in the *Morning Post* and studying the latest fashion plates. Alicia would never have been seen wearing a frayed riding habit, Kitty thought sadly. She wished some of Alicia's instinctive knowledge would rub off on her, but no matter how hard she tried to emulate her, she always forgot Alicia's lessons at the crucial moment.

Their father was delighted to see Kitty in the room. "I thought we'd have to wait for you, as usual, my dear," he said, kissing her cheek and not noticing her hair. "Just when I've got such splendid surprises for you all." He reached into his pocket to pull out his spectacles and some papers. "Where are Nellie and Timothy? Don't they know what time dinner is served?"

At this point, the door opened and the two missing children entered. Nellie, fourteen years old, and Timothy, thirteen, came into the room. They resembled each other very strongly, as did all the four youngest children. They had the same

45

brown eyes and fair hair and complexion that their father had had in his youth. They were built much the same as he was, too: tall and thin. And they moved with an easy grace. Kitty, on the other hand, resembled her mother. She was small, with dark hair, blue eyes, and clear white skin. She was bursting with energy and rarely took the time to appear graceful. Because she resembled her mother's family so strongly, she was named after her grandmother, Mary Kathleen Conally, who chose to repay this honor by leaving most of her considerable fortune to Kitty. How she had amassed it was never clearly known, but there were many speculations about it. Most agreed it was not acquired legally. This did not bother Kitty's father, though, who had great respect for money, wherever it came from.

Their father put his spectacles on and looked at the papers he held. "As I was saying, I have some surprises for you all." He was clearly bursting with news. "I have invited your Aunt Mavis to come and stay with us for a few weeks." No one said anything, so he continued. "Today I received a letter from Lord Scotney asking leave to visit us next week to make final preparations for the wedding." Satisfied that Kitty was not about to make an unladylike remark, because she appeared to be in shock, he went on. "He says that he had hoped to arrive sooner, but he is anxious to prepare Scotney Park for your coming, Kitty. Your aunt will act as hostess for us when we entertain him." He looked over at Kitty, who seemed to be recovering her voice. He hurried on to avoid any comment she might decide to make. "She has been in London and hoped to visit us soon anyway, so I told her to plan on the next few weeks here. I'm going up to town to pick her up the day after tomorrow. That should give us plenty of time to prepare for the big arrival, eh, Kitty?"

In his excitement, he obviously forgot Kitty's feelings toward the whole thing. Everyone sat waiting to see what Kitty would do with the opening her father had given her. They didn't have to wait long.

"You can prepare all you like for the 'big arrival,'" she said. "But all you'll do is tell him that your daughter refuses to marry him."

William Tolbert rose, his face getting very red. "You'll do as you're told, girl, and you've been told for the past ten years that you were going to marry the Earl of Scotney when you came of age. You should have married him last year, and you would have but for the war with the Frenchies. Well, there's no stopping it this time. It's going ahead as planned."

"No, it's not going ahead as *you've* planned. I have planned differently, and I don't intend to marry Claude. I detest him, I despise him, I hold him in the greatest contempt. I will never marry him." Kitty could shout as loud as her father.

The others were watching in awe. None of them had any real gumption when it came to standing up to their father, and they enjoyed a good battle when one came along. But they knew, no matter how well Kitty argued, she would eventually lose. Their father always got his way.

"Well," her father said strangely, "actually you don't have to marry Claude."

Kitty was aware he wasn't giving in to her wishes. She knew him too well for that. But she did wonder what game he was playing. She was silent for a few moments.

"Actually," he said, "Claude was killed a few months ago. It's his brother you're going to marry. He's the Earl now. I got a letter from their lawyer explaining it all. It seems the brother is very anxious to abide by the contract. He's hoping to get things settled soon." William was quite expert at twisting the truth around to suit his purpose.

"His brother!" Kitty shouted. "Who is his brother? You're marrying me off to somebody we have never even heard of. Somebody we know nothing about. That's even worse than Claude. At least I knew what he was like. You could always pretend that he cared about me . . . but a stranger! All he wants is my money and to even the debt off to you. It all boils down to money! You know nothing about him, do you?" she accused.

William was used to getting his own way and would not tolerate being crossed. "Of course I know something about him. He's the Earl of Scotney, now that his father is dead," he yelled back.

"So you're selling me for a title, is that it? Anything to get a title in the family. Well, you can't force me to marry him. I'll lock myself in my room first. I'll run away." Kitty was searching her mind for a really dire threat, but she was so angry that nothing really good came to mind.

"Never!" she contented herself with, and charged out of the room.

William followed her to the hall. "You'll do as I say, Mary Kathleen Tolbert!" he shouted after her. Then he stomped into his study.

The butler, after quietly removing two places at the table, came into the drawing room to announce that dinner was ready.

CHAPTER THREE

William Tolbert was still in a foul mood the next morning. He ate early, before any of his children were awake, and went out to the stables to find his horse ready for his morning exercise. A good fast run over the downs—that should clear his thinking.

As he rode, he went over the events that had led up to the previous night's disagreement. He knew that Kitty felt he was being unreasonable to insist on this marriage, but he really believed it would be best for her. Even when Kitty was very young he could see how she resembled her mother's family, not just in looks, but in her impetuous and willful behavior. It could easily lead her into trouble, and he was determined to prevent that.

Alicia and Nellie he could understand. They were much more like him, and though they'd hate to admit it, very much like his sister, Mavis. They wouldn't let their emotions override their good sense, no matter what they thought now. If the occasion arose, he knew all the training they had had would lead them in the right direction.

What Kitty needed was someone who would be responsible for her. Someone other than her father, William thought. Although he did love her, he wouldn't be sorry to see her married and living somewhere else. Since her mother died five years ago, it had been harder and harder to keep Kitty in line. Of course, William had to admit that Mary might not have been able to do it either, had she lived. But she had approved of the betrothal to Lord Scotney. She thought it would be just the thing for Kitty.

William was honest enough with himself to realize that the title weighed heavily with him. He could remember his mother, whom he had idolized, being snubbed by the gentry near their home. Her father had been in trade, a seemingly unpardonable sin. Even though William's father was almost without funds, he was widely received until he married William's mother, who had been quite wealthy. Then they were severely ostracized.

It got slightly better, in time, but his mother was never truly accepted, and neither were her children.

He did not want his children to suffer like that. His great ambition was to have them accepted by leaders of society in London. He'd like to give the younger girls a season there to get them well established. This betrothal was just the thing to accomplish that.

By the time William returned to the house, he was no longer angry at Kitty, just more convinced than ever that she needed a firmer hand than his to control her. He went cheerfully into the house, where he spent the morning closeted with his agent.

When Kitty heard her father leave the house that morning, she raced downstairs. She had been up for nearly an hour, waiting for him to go, because she wasn't anxious to meet him. She realized that she made a fatal mistake last night in arguing with him. That never got her anywhere with her father. He would refuse to budge the minute he realized he was being crossed. What she had to do now was to think things out on her own and decide on the best way to foil his plans. The first thing to do was to eat breakfast.

After a large meal, Kitty felt able to cope with anything, and she was wishing that Lord Scotney himself would come riding up to the house so she could tell him just what she thought of somebody who married a person, without even seeing her, just because she had money. She dwelt happily on how she would verbally slay him, while waiting for her sisters.

After breakfast the three of them changed into riding habits for their normal morning ride. Alicia was a far better rider than the other two, and she quickly outdistanced them. Nellie probably could have caught up with her, but Kitty called her back to tell her of her adventures of the day before. Nellie was most interested in Kitty's handsome rescuer and thought it was all terribly romantic. She did not, however, approve of her sister's lack of skill on a horse.

"Well, it all sounds terribly nice, except the part about you falling off Dancer. How can anything romantic happen to you if you can't even stay on a horse?" Nellie watched her sister riding slightly ahead of her. Kitty was slipping in the saddle. "You really ought to make more of an effort to stay on."

Alicia joined them in time to hear Nellie's last remark. "It's true, Kitty," she agreed. "You aren't a very good rider. But perhaps the Earl will buy you a curricle and pair to drive in the park. I'm not sure you could handle a very spirited pair, but you will have to be seen there, you know. When I come to visit you, perhaps you'll let me take the ribbons for a spell. I would dearly love to tool through Hyde Park. Think of all the handsome gentlemen you'll meet there, Kitty."

"Well, I'll be married by the time I'm 'tooling around the park,' so I don't see what difference the handsome men will make," Kitty said dryly.

"What a ninny you are, Kitty," Alicia said in disgust. "Don't you know anything? You have to meet some handsome men. Who else will escort you to parties and balls and to the theater? Every married woman has them, or she'd never go anywhere."

"Won't her husband object if she's with other men?" Nellie wanted to know.

Alicia was surprised at her sisters' lack of worldly knowledge. "After she gives him an heir, he won't care what she does as long as she's discreet."

"Discreet about what?" Kitty wanted to know.

"About taking lovers, what else?" Alicia said, astonished that she would even have to ask. "He'll be busy with his own flirts anyway, other married women and widows, so he wouldn't bother you much. Why I read that sometimes a husband and wife can go for weeks without seeing one another except if they're invited to the same party. Then they might have a chance to exchange a few words." She laughed at Kitty's and Nellie's shocked faces. "You two are unbelievable. I can understand that Nellie wouldn't know all this, but you should, Kitty; you're eighteen already. You had better catch up with the world or your husband is going to be terribly disgusted with your naiveté. What did you expect a marriage of convenience was? It's most convenient for both sides because you each get to go your own way. I think it sounds ideal, and so will you, once you grow up." She turned her horse away, as if she was too sophisticated to bear their company any longer, and rode back to the house.

"Do you think that all that was true?" Nellie whispered to Kitty. "Maybe she was making it up to shock us. She does that sometimes, you know."

"No, I think it was all true. She does know a lot more about the way people live in London, you know. I just never paid much attention to gossip, so it's all new to me."

"It doesn't sound like the way I'd like to live," Nellie said defiantly. "I'm going to marry somebody who loves me."

"I think you've been reading too many novels, Nellie. It doesn't sound like anybody marries for love these days."

Nellie was disturbed by the defeated look on Kitty's face. "It's not like you to give up so easily," she said. "I should think you'd be willing to fight against a marriage like that. You know you aren't the type to have lovers and turn your back on your husband and his affairs. You'd hate that."

"Oh, I haven't given up yet," Kitty reassured Nellie. "I'm more determined than ever to get out of this engagement. I'll think of a plan before it's too late, I promise you."

William left for London early the next morning. He had some business to attend to, then he would meet Mavis and bring her back with him. They were expected to return late the following day, but Kitty was not anxious for them to arrive. Her aunt would do anything she was told to do, and she certainly would never dream of supporting Kitty in going against her father's wishes.

Soon after Kitty heard her father's carriage pull away, she came down the stairs. She drifted into the dining room, but she didn't have much appetite for the breakfast put in front of her. In spite of the brave front she had assumed for Nellie's sake, Kitty was quite worried. Lord Scotney was expected a few days after her father's return, and she had no idea how she could successfully oppose her father's plan.

She was picking aimlessly at her food when Alicia and Nellie came in. Alicia was obviously bursting with plans.

"It's raining too hard to go for a ride this morning, so I thought we could study some of the new fashion plates," she said. "Father was saying last night that you would need quite a lot for your trousseau, so we could start making lists." She took a drink of her chocolate and added in a low voice, "He is expecting Aunt Mavis to help, but I think we would do better to get as much done before she comes as we can. She would dress you abominably, you know. She wouldn't choose the right things at all, but I'm sure that we can get her to agree to the things we pick out."

Alicia went on listing her plans while she ate steadily. She was finished long before the others.

"When you've eaten, come up to the sitting room. I'll get things ready for us." She jumped up and ran from the room.

"Well, she certainly is excited," Nellie said.

"All these fashion plans are her idea of heaven. She's going to force all her ideas on us, you know."

Kitty nodded. "She ought to be planning all that for herself, not me. She'd make a good, convenient countess."

Nellie made a face. "Are you still bothered by the things she said yesterday? She might be wrong, you know. Maybe you'll fall in love with your Earl the minute you see him. Wouldn't that be romantic?"

"Face it, Nellie. Romance isn't going to enter into this, and, personally, I'd prefer never to even see the Earl." Kitty stood up. "Hurry and finish. You can't leave me to face Alicia all by myself."

Kitty left the room, and Nellie, gulping down her chocolate, followed soon after.

The morning was spent arguing over the merits of silks, satins, velvets, and muslins. No one suggested a continuation of the planning after luncheon. Kitty announced she was going for a ride because it had stopped raining, and she left before anyone could offer to go with her. She was terribly fond of Nellie, but she felt a real need to be by herself and do some thinking. She refused to submit tamely to this marriage and was determined to find a way out of it.

The stable hands were so engrossed in conversation that she thought she would have to saddle her horse by herself.

"What's all the excitement about?" she asked.

"There's a horse fair near Draybly," one of them said. "Some buyers from London are comin' out and they're looking for local stock to buy. There's to be jumping and racin' to show how good the horses are."

"How long is this fair going to be at Draybly?" she asked.

By this time, two other hands had come over, and were quite willing to share all they knew about it with their young mistress.

"I think today's the last day," one said.

"No, t'ain't," another was sure. "Bailey said he weren't goin' till tomorrow."

"That's right," a third agreed. "Its to run through tomorrow at least."

"But it'd be over for sure before your pa could take you there, if he had a mind to." They all nodded wisely, sure that Mr. Tolbert was not likely to take his daughter there even if he had been home.

Kitty rode off thinking, remembering Nellie's comments from the previous day. It was true. How could she hope for something exciting and romantic to happen to her when she couldn't even stay on a horse! The more she thought about the fair, the more she wanted to go. She enjoyed riding. She wasn't completely mad for it like some girls she had met, but she did wish that she could ride better. The very first romantic novel that she had ever read ended with the hero and heroine riding off across the moors together. Since she had been only thirteen, and rather impressionable, she decided the picture of them riding away together was the most romantic thing imaginable.

Since that time, she had been struggling to improve her riding, so that when her hero came along, she would be able to ride off across the moors with him without falling off. The fact that she did not live near any moors and that she had supposedly matured since then did nothing to diminish her belief that good riding was a necessary ingredient for romance.

This fair was a terrific chance for her. She was sure that if she saw some really good jumpers she would be fired with determination and would have the courage she needed. All she had to do was to figure out a way to get to the show.

Kitty found a place near the creek to sit. She dismounted and tied Dancer loosely to a nearby bush. She sat down, watching the water rush over the rocks, while the horse started grazing. She couldn't ride over to it by herself. Neither would a groom or Willy be chaperone enough. She wondered if the horse fair would be a proper place for a young girl no matter how well accompanied she was. It wasn't fair that Willy could go practically anyplace he wanted, while she was so bound by convention. But suppose, she thought, she was to pretend to be Willy. Who would know she was a girl if she dressed like him? It was an awfully daring thing to do, but no one would pay much attention to a young schoolboy at a horse show. Kitty was nervous at the mere thought of appearing in boys' clothes, but the idea of actually being able to go to the show overcame any objections she could think of. Heroines in her novels were doing it all the time, she thought, so why couldn't she?

CHAPTER FOUR

The next morning everything went according to Kitty's plan. She told her sisters that she was visiting Letty Winfield, a neighbor with whom she often spent the day. She wore an old riding habit with a loose-fitting jacket over an old shirt of her brother's. Under the full skirt, she wore a less than distinguished pair of breeches. They smelled very strongly of horses, but they were the only ones that she could find that would fit her. She didn't think that the smell would be particularly noticeable once she got to the show. She managed to throw an old saddle on Dancer and led her away from the house. Once concealed by trees, she pulled off her skirt and hid it beneath a low bush. The wind was blowing her hair into her face, so she tied it securely back with a ribbon and pulled a dusty old cap low over her face. She mounted Dancer and started off on what she was sure would be a great adventure.

Kitty had left home with the idea of arriving in

Draybly around nine o'clock. She didn't know what time the show would start, but since she had to be home before her father, she decided to stay for whatever the show offered early and leave around midday. She had brought some money and occasionally patted her pockets to reassure herself it was still there. It was only for emergencies, because she had packed a lunch to eat on the way home. Kitty was so excited about her day out that she almost forgot about her father and Lord Scotney. In her present optimistic mood, she was confident that a solution to all her problems would present itself soon, and she was not about to spend her whole day worrying.

After she had ridden for about an hour, Kitty was wishing it was not so bright and sunny. She was terribly hot and uncomfortable. She would have dearly loved to take off her jacket, but she didn't dare. Once she reached the place where the show was held, she would find a cool spot to relax —maybe even get a drink of lemonade or cider.

Kitty reached Draybly about the time she had planned. There weren't too many people around. She didn't want to ask directions because she was feeling very self-conscious and hesitated to call attention to herself. She wondered how all those women in books got away with wearing boys' clothes. She felt very conspicuous in them and suspected that everyone who glanced at her knew the truth.

She had convinced herself, while riding along, that she ought to be able to find the show by herself. Surely, there would be a number of people going there. All she would have to do is follow them. By ten o'clock, she was tired of waiting. The only crowd she had seen was four men going to a farm to see the damage done by a fire the night before. Finally, she saw an old man walking along the dusty road away from town. She asked him about the fair, only to learn that it had left several days ago.

"Yure friends musta had it wrong," he said, "Ain't here no more." With that he turned away and continued down the road.

She was so hot and disappointed that she felt like crying.

"Well, Dancer, I guess it's back home again," she said, turning her horse around, but the road back lay uninvitingly in front of her.

"Let's cut across these fields," she said to her horse. "It won't save any time, but it's not so hot there." She turned Dancer off the road, and they started off across a low meadow, through long patches of shade under huge oak trees. It wasn't as easy going as she had thought, and Dancer was longing for a run.

"Well, go ahead, then," she said, giving her her head, "but you're to watch for holes."

Dancer raced across the field, along some paths, and through some open gates. She didn't see anyone the whole time, but she thought that this land must be in use, because of the gates.

"Do you think we ought to go back and close the gates?" she asked Dancer, who kept right on going. "I guess that whoever opened them wanted them open," she reasoned. Since she had seen no stock, she wasn't concerned. As they ran, Kitty caught glimpses of the road, usually alongside them, occasionally in front of them. Finally, she saw the trees ahead were thicker, and she realized that they had to return to the road. She looked for a gate to get them back to it but didn't see one.

"Am I going to have to go all the way back?" she asked herself. Dancer had slowed down considerably and, feeling her indecision, stopped. She turned her slightly, trying to see the entire length of the fence near them, when she spotted movement across the field. She watched for a few seconds as an animal came toward them. Dancer reared and she brought her back down, realizing that they had entered a bull's grazing area, and the bull was charging toward them.

Kitty did not give in to panic, but neither was she thinking clearly. Her only thought was to get back to the road, so she headed Dancer toward it. The horse took off, then Kitty saw the fence looming ahead. Dancer, it was obvious, was going over. Kitty held on tight and prayed she'd go over, too. But at the last minute, she let go, knowing she couldn't do it. Her fear of jumping the fence had obliterated everything else from her mind. When she hit the ground, the memory of the bull came back and she scrambled under the fence, just in time. She could feel hot breath right behind her. She moved away from the fence quickly and sat down by the road until she could stop shaking.

Dancer was drinking from a puddle next to the road and nibbling grass that was near it. Except for her heaving sides, Dancer looked as though she was just out for a morning trot. Kitty had no inclination to move, but there were some horses coming, and she felt silly sitting there.

She walked stiffly over to Dancer and pulled her away from the puddle, looking for something to use as a mounting block. As she walked beside the horse Kitty noticed Dancer was limping.

"Oh, dear," she said. "Did you hurt your leg?" No, she wasn't hurt, but she had thrown a shoe and couldn't be ridden until it was replaced.

"Well, I guess we're both walking," she told her horse.

Holding the reins, she started down the road. The sun got hotter as it got higher, and Kitty was sorry she had ever started out. This was not the exciting adventure she had thought it would be. She was hot, dirty, and dying of thirst. Willy's boots were awful. She was just debating whether she'd be better off barefoot, when she saw a curricle approaching.

She pulled Dancer off to the side of the road and continued her debate. She wasn't aware that the horses had pulled up beside her until she heard a voice speaking to her.

"Can I offer you a lift someplace?" a man was asking.

She looked up and saw, looking down at her, the

63

stranger who had helped her by the creek. Of all the people she didn't want to meet looking like this, he had to top the list.

"What happened to your horse?" he asked.

"She threw a shoe," Kitty explained. "I have to walk her back."

"Where to?"

"Near Crofton."

"That's a long walk," he said.

"I don't mind it," Kitty told him.

He smiled. "Your feet seem to."

She knew he must have seen her limping along the road as he approached. He moved over on the seat, and she climbed up after tying Dancer to the back. He didn't speak to her at first because he was trying to go around a farm wagon that was stopped on the road, so Kitty made use of the time to decide on her plan of action. She thought it would be best to play the part she was dressed for. Surely, as a gentleman he wouldn't be too inquisitive. But then she wasn't an expert on how gentlemen behaved toward schoolboys or toward girls who dressed like them.

"Out for a morning ride?" Robin asked.

"Yes, sir," she answered, trying to make her voice sound harsh.

"Robin," he said, extending his hand. "Robin Prentice."

"Hello," Kitty said, taking his hand uncertainly. "I'm Kit. Kit . . . Conally." Well, after all, that wasn't a lie. Her name was Mary Kathleen Conally Tolbert, but she didn't have to tell him that.

"Glad to know you, Kit. You on holiday from school?" he asked.

"Yes, sir," she said. "I've got a few more days before the next term starts.

"Robin," he said. In answer to her puzzled look, he added, "It makes me feel very old to be called 'Sir'; you can't be that much younger than me." He smiled at her and looked even younger. Somehow she didn't think it was right to call a young man by his given name, but to refuse would certainly seem strange.

There seemed to be a lot of traffic on the road, so they didn't have much chance to talk, a fact that Kitty was quite greatful for. Although she had seen him give her a few curious glances, he didn't mention their previous encounter or seem to doubt that she was who she said she was. Maybe he had forgotten or just didn't recognize her.

Robin had not forgotten the girl whom he had met near the creek that day. Much as he tried to put her out of his mind, he found it impossible. That was the type of girl, he told himself, that he would have chosen to marry. Not some stiff-necked spinster who had a lot of money. She wasn't ashamed that her clothes were worn. Neither was she a stiff, lifeless maiden, without conversation, dressed up to attract a husband, like many young girls he had seen in London. She was real and full of life, and he could kick himself (as he had, mentally, quite often since meeting her) that he hadn't even learned her name.

He had immediately recognized the striking re-

65

semblance between her and the youth next to him. He debated asking him right out about her, but he didn't want to give the wrong impression. You just didn't start discussing a young lady with a stranger. Besides, there was always the possibility that she hadn't mentioned the incident, and he wouldn't want to cause her any trouble. He was about to throw in a seemingly innocent question about Kit's family when he was hailed from behind him.

"Robin! Robin! Pull up, boy." Robin turned and saw Sir Matthew Trilby and Tom Wentworth in a curricle behind him. Riding next to them was Peter Marwood, a cousin of Trilby who was in his first year at Oxford. They quickly pulled alongside him. "Robin! This is really lucky. We were hoping you'd get away to meet us here." Tom called to him.

"How's the park?" Trilby wanted to know. "Everything in shape for the big day?"

"As ready as it'll ever be," Robin frowned. "I hope Julian's been busy."

"He'll be there, don't worry." Trilby was positive.

It was Peter who first noticed the silent youth next to Robin.

"Who's the friend, Robin?" he asked, nodding toward Kitty. Robin had not forgotten Kit but was trying to figure out how he could still get his undisturbed talk with him now that he'd met up with his friends. Well, that would have to be worked out later, he thought, as he introduced Kit to his friends.

"Is he coming with us?" Tom wanted to know.

"Sure, why not," said Peter. "Ever been to a cockfight?" he asked Kitty.

"No," said Kitty, "and I don't think I'd better go with you . . ."

"Nonsense," interrupted Trilby, "you look too old never to have been to a cockfight. It's high time you got started. Right, Robin?"

"No, really," insisted Kitty. "Robin never meant to bring me. He just offered me a ride. I don't want to intrude."

"You're not intrudin', lad," Trilby told him. "We're glad to have you along."

"But I really don't want to see a cockfight," Kitty pleaded, feeling quite desperate to get away.

"You're not squeamish, are you?" asked Peter in disgust.

Of course I am, thought Kitty, but when it was put like that what could she say? It was a little late to announce that she was a well-bred girl of eighteen and had no place at a cockfight, let alone in the company of four strange men.

"No, I am not squeamish," Kitty said defiantly. "I just have to be getting home."

"You wouldn't get home very quickly if you were walking," Robin pointed out. "I'll take you back to Crofton right after the fight, and you'll still get there sooner than you would have if you had walked." Robin was reluctant to let the boy leave without finding out any more about him and his family. He was not likely to get another opportunity like this.

There was very little Kitty could do except demand that the horses be stopped, get out, untie Dancer, and walk off. It might be best if she just endured the next few hours somehow and then went home. There was little chance that she would see any of them again, so if she could make it through the fight itself she would be safe.

All too soon, Robin turned the curricle down a side road. He was aware of his companion's agitation and was a little sorry he had forced the issue, but he really did want to talk to him. He smiled to himself when he remembered his first cockfight. He hadn't liked it much, but then he didn't like them a great deal now. It was a place to go that his meager budget would allow, and they always had a good time afterwards. He would have liked to reassure him that it wouldn't last long, but thought that Kit might prefer his nervousness to go unnoticed.

There were not too many horses and carriages around the field where the fight was to take place.

"We're pretty early," said Tom. "Let's go back to that inn."

They left their horses and curricules in the care of a rather surly boy who brightened up at the coins that Trilby tossed to him.

The inside of the inn was no more cheerful than the outside, and Kitty hoped the glasses would be cleaner than the windows. The coffee room was already crowded, but Robin managed to find them a space at the long table in the center while Trilby went in search of the proprietor. Trilby came back a few minutes later, trying to carry five tankards of ale without spilling them. Kitty looked with dismay at the one put in front of her. She was about to say she'd prefer lemonade when she caught Peter watching her. He seemed determined to make her appear childish. Now he was waiting for her to make some objection to the ale. Well, she'd show him she was no green schoolboy.

Trilby held up his glass. "Here's to Tom and his beautiful bride-to-be. May she keep him warm in the cold of Northumberland." Tom turned a bright red, to everyone's great amusement, while they all drank deeply. Kitty made an effort not to gasp when she swallowed. How people drank ale she didn't know, it tasted awful.

"I hear that Robin is next on the list to be married," Peter said. When no one responded, he asked, "Shouldn't we toast his bride also?" Robin and Trilby looked embarrassed, while Tom looked rather confused.

After a moment, Trilby said, a little too jovially, "Here's wishing you happy, Robin." They all drank quickly, anxious to be off an unaccountably uncomfortable topic.

Kitty might have wondered why Robin and Trilby were so uneasy when Robin's upcoming marriage was mentioned, but she was too busy wondering why the thought of it left her so depressed. It's ridiculous she told herself. For all she had known about Robin, he might already have been married and be the father of ten children. Her logical reasoning did not improve her mood, though.

Trilby noticed people leaving the room, and he jumped at the excuse. "We'd better get out there if we want good seats."

Kitty would have preferred some really bad seats, but she couldn't think of an excuse to delay them.

They all left the inn and crowded around the ring where the fight was to take place. Even though there were a number of people already assembled, Trilby pushed his way to the front and found places for them all. Kitty looked cautiously around, but she didn't see anyone she knew. Thank God that Willy didn't go to these events; though, if he showed up, at least he could take her home. But the thought of Willy taking her home instead of Robin only made her more unhappy.

Suddenly, there was a great commotion as some of the men started making bets and the birds were brought into the ring. One was bright red, with a brown streak down its back. The other was pure white. It was bigger than the red bird, but Trilby said he wasn't necessarily the best fighter.

"I'll back the Spanish Red any day," he said, trying to get one of them to bet against him.

"Want to bet on the white?" he asked Kitty.

Peter was watching her, suspiciously, Kitty thought, so she felt she ought to make some sort of show and reached for her purse. She searched one pocket, then another, only to find each was empty.

"I've lost my purse," she said to Trilby. "I can't find it anywhere."

She must have dropped it when she fell off Dancer. She hadn't thought to check her pockets after she climbed under the fence, although even if she had seen it where she fell, she wouldn't have fought the bull to gain possession of it.

"Do you think someone stole it here?" Trilby asked. There were a lot of suspicious-looking creatures about, but he didn't think that he had the muscle to back up an accusation.

"Are you sure you lost it here?" Robin asked, thinking along the same lines as Trilby.

"No," Kitty said. "I fell when my horse jumped a fence, and I must have dropped it then. That's when he lost his shoe."

Robin's eyes narrowed as he took a better look at Kitty. Surely the whole family could not be afflicted with a fear of jumping fences. A commotion in the ring as it was being prepared for the fight distracted Robin's attention from her, and Kitty was relieved. It was not pleasant to be stranded here without funds, but it was equally frightening to realize that Robin was getting suspicious of her. She began to wish fervently that she had never come, which did no good in helping her to get back home. Then the fight began.

Kitty could not have imagined how awful it would be. The cocks kept biting and clawing at each other, while the men cheered them on. When the red bird viciously bit the other bird's neck, there was a burst of clapping and laughter. The white bird was soon streaked with blood. Kitty closed her eyes. She didn't care if Peter saw her and thought she was lily-livered; she just prayed she wouldn't faint or disgrace herself.

As much as she could shut out the sight, she couldn't shut out the screaming of the birds or the cheering of the men. Suddenly Kitty knew she had to get out of there. Not caring what anybody thought of her, she climbed over Robin and pushed through the crowd, losing her cap. Once free of them, she raced away from the noise, around the back of the inn to the shade of some bushes. It was far enough away that she could hear only sporadic bursts of yelling. She sank down on the ground and put her face on her knees.

Once the nausea and dizziness passed, she picked her head up. Robin was standing right in front of her, watching her with a strange look on his face. She took a deep breath, wondering if he was so still because she had embarrassed him by leaving. Surely he wouldn't make a big deal of that; after all, what business was it of his if she couldn't stomach cockfights?

Her hair had fallen over her face and she reached up to push it out of the way, but Robin caught hold of her wrist. She looked at him questioningly, but he was staring at her hand. She looked at it, also. She could still see the places where she had been scratched by the bramble bush several days ago.

Any hope that he might not know the truth died when she saw his face. He said nothing, but his face was very white and stern, and his eyes were cold. He tightened his hold on her, then dragged her behind him to his curricle. He half-lifted, half-threw her onto the seat. Then he jumped up himself and swiftly guided his horses away from the others. Kitty sneaked a look at him while he was turning onto the road. His face was still as white and stern as it had been. She wondered why he was so angry with her, and, stifling a small sob, she turned away.

Robin was indeed very angry and didn't trust himself to speak. His anger was not directed against Kitty, as she thought, but against himself. She had very clearly stated that she didn't want to go to the fight, but he had insisted. He was so determined to talk with her that the thought that she might be the very girl he was looking for had never occurred to him. It was his stubbornness that had led her into a very damning position. When he thought of the problems that could have confronted her had she been discovered or seen by anyone other than himself, he felt like letting his horses trample all over him. But that wouldn't help her now. What he had to do was make sure she was all right, then get her home as fast as possible.

About a mile away from the site of the fight, there was a small grassy area under some trees. He pulled off the road and stopped the horses under the trees. Robin jumped out and began rummaging under the seat. Kitty watched him for a minute, but he seemed determined not to meet her eyes. She climbed down and went to sit in the shade. She still felt very shaky, and it was a relief to sit where it was cool. Robin followed her with a small basket in one hand and a flask in the other. He poured a small glass of some amber-colored liquid and handed it to her. She looked at it hesitantly.

"Drink it," he said, in a voice that left no room for argument.

She did but started to cough as the fiery stuff went down.

"Well," Robin smiled slightly. "At least you're not a hardened drinker yet."

He opened the basket and took out some food. There was bread, cold meats, and some fruit. He started eating some of it and told her to do the same, but he didn't seem to be paying much attention to whether she did or not.

Kitty took an apple and tried to eat it. After ale and what she guessed was brandy, her stomach wasn't receptive to the idea of food. She had to force herself to eat it. By the time it was gone, Robin had finished all that he wanted and was watching her.

"Do you feel better now?" he asked.

She nodded.

"Well, Kit . . ." he stopped. "Is it Kit?"

"Kitty," she said.

"Well, Kitty, I'd like to know what you were doing out dressed like that and going to a cockfight."

At the mention of the fight she went pale again. "I told you I didn't want to go there," she said defensively.

"All right, I'll admit that, but what were you doing out like that in the first place? Don't you have any sense?" He was not going to be distracted from his main point.

"I wanted to see the horse show in Draybly," she said, as if that explained everything.

"My God!" he exploded. "You can't just dress up like that and go off by yourself. Do you know what kind of trouble you could have gotten into? Do you know what could have happened had you been discovered by someone other than me?"

She looked slightly uncomfortable, but Robin was not through yet. He was just getting warmed up to his subject. He rose and began to pace up and down in front of her.

"How old are you anyway?" he asked.

"Eighteen."

"Good Lord," he said, stopping in front of her. "You're no schoolgirl. Do you know what people would have thought had they known that I had a woman with me there? A woman who dressed herself up like that?" He pointed at her clothes.

At that, Kitty jumped up and glared at him. Robin had the feeling that he had taken the wrong tactic somewhere.

"So that's what's really bothering you, isn't it?" She walked over to where he was standing. She glared at him. Her anger made him feel he ought to apologize, but when he was standing so close to her all he wanted to do was pull her into his arms and kiss her. The realization of this last wish so surprised him that he could do nothing for the moment.

"Are you so angry because you had to leave the fight early, or are you afraid of what your fiancée might say if she knew you were with me?" Through all the horrors of the fight, Kitty was still bothered by the fact that he was engaged to be married.

"Well, you needn't worry. I'm not going to tell any of this to anybody. If we should ever meet again, which is unlikely because I don't plan to attend any more cockfights, we can easily pretend that we've never met. If you would please take me back to Crofton, I won't embarrass you any more with my presence."

She turned away and said more quietly, "For your information, I was sorry long ago that I came out today. All I wanted was to get back home. It was not my idea to go to that horrible fight."

She went to where the cloth was spread out. She picked up the food that was left and packed it into the basket. After putting it under the seat, she climbed up.

Robin was still standing where she left him. She seems to think the discussion is at an end, he thought, the way she's sitting there so stiffly and staring straight ahead. There were still a few things he would say, he told himself grimly, getting in after her, and he would say them even if he had to gag her to get a chance to speak.

"You are deliberately misunderstanding me," he said as the horses gained the road once more. "I am not concerned about what anybody might think of me. Except for your father, who would want to skin me alive, no one would think less of me for being with you. It's your reputation that I'm worried about."

Kitty was still staring straight ahead. She was devoutly wishing that she had never embarked on her adventure and didn't want to hear any more about it from Robin. She was in no mood for a lecture, and it certainly didn't help that he was so infuriatingly right about the whole thing.

Robin was not daunted by her silence, though. Rather, it encouraged him to expound on the dangers of her situation.

"No well-brought-up young lady would do something like this. Do you know what kind of woman those men would have thought you were? They would have thought I had picked up some . . ." Too late he realized where his thoughts were taking him. He was venturing on ground that was totally unsuitable for a conversation with a young lady.

"Fancy piece?" Kitty supplied for him.

"Well, they would think you were awfully fast," Robin finished lamely.

"Would your fiancée mind that you had picked up some horribly fast female?" Kitty asked, not consciously changing the subject, but actually very curious about the woman Robin was to marry.

Robin was not against a new topic, because he

felt that he hadn't handled the last one very well, but he would have preferred any other subject than the one Kitty had chosen.

"She would not care what I did, as long as I did not die before the wedding," he said.

"That's a horrible thing to say," Kitty cried. "It makes it sound like she doesn't care about you at all."

"She doesn't," said Robin, matter-of-factly.

"If she doesn't love you, why is she marrying you then?"

"Kitty," Robin said in exasperation, "people very rarely marry for love, except in Mrs. Radcliffe's novels, and judging by your behavior, I'd say you've read far too many of them."

"You don't sound like you care about her either," Kitty said, ignoring the forbidding look on his face.

"For heaven's sake," Robin hissed at her. "So I'm not madly in love with her. What difference does that make? You make it sound like a crime to marry someone I'm not in love with. How do you know we won't be happy together?"

My God, thought Robin. Here I am defending the travesty of a marriage that I'd do anything to get out of. But he couldn't divulge the true circumstances of his betrothal, to Kitty. He was too ashamed of it himself to want anyone else to know the truth about it.

"Maybe you'll grow to love her after you're married," Kitty suggested in a small voice.

"Stop kidding yourself, Kitty. Love doesn't always go along with marriage. And I'm not about to fall in love with her."

"How can you be so sure?" Kitty persisted.

"I'm not going to, that's all," said Robin, giving her a quelling glance that ordered her to stop.

She ignored it and pushed further. "Well, it could happen, you know. You might really get to be fond of her. It's not impossible."

"I think it's quite impossible for me to fall in love with her if I'm already in love with someone else." As soon as he said it, Robin knew that it was true. That was why he couldn't forget the grubby young girl he had rescued from the bushes, why he jumped at the chance to find out more about her, and why he was so angry when she had been in such a compromising position.

Robin always felt he was a basically honorable person, but now, faced with the realization that he was in love with one girl while pledged to marry another, he wondered if honor was such a worthwhile thing to have. If Kitty returned his love, couldn't they find a way to be together? He pictured them just riding right through Crofton and on to a new life together. Or was that being as romantic as he had accused Kitty of being? One look at Kitty's face told him she was not sharing his dreams.

"You mean you're in love with someone else, but you're still going to marry this poor woman? That's disgusting!"

Robin decided that it might be the wrong time to broach the subject of just who the other woman was. He'd better first clear up her strange idea of his betrothal.

"It's not as if my fiancée and I care about each other." He stumbled ahead, even though she was looking more and more shocked with each word. "There were reasons why we chose to become engaged. She does not expect, or probably want, any affection from me."

"It's just a marriage of convenience, then," said Kitty in a deceptively quiet voice.

"Yes, that's all it would be," said Robin, relieved that she was understanding that part so well.

"I know all about them," she said in a not-so-quiet voice. "Alicia told me all about them."

"Who's Alicia?" he asked, momentarily diverted.

She ignored him. "I suppose you've got your married ladies and your widows all picked out, haven't you?"

"What?" Robin felt like he had missed something vital in the conversation.

She went on as if he hadn't spoken. "Of course," she said in the tone of one making an important discovery, "your true love must be one of them. I suppose she is very attractive and amusing."

"No, more like confusing," inserted Robin, catching an occasional glimmer of what Kitty was talking about.

Kitty glared at him. "I don't think it's very funny," she said, and to his horror, he saw that she was close to tears. "I think it's hateful. It's not what a marriage should be."

"Now, wait a minute, Kitty," said Robin.

"I thought you were nice, but you're just like the rest of them," she cried.

He decided that a little plain talking might be in order, and because Kitty was starting to hiccough from the tears running down her face, he thought that this might be his chance to explain without interruption.

"You see," he began, "my father really got me into . . ." But he never got the chance to finish, for at that moment the London-Brighton coach came careening around the bend toward them. Robin had to pull his horses far to the side to let it pass.

Unfortunately, at the same moment a farm wagon, loaded high with hay, was planning on crossing the road. The farm horse, usually docile in disposition, took affront at the many horses and carriages in his normally peaceful area. He tried to speed up and veered to the side. This was not a wise move, for the wagon was not made very strongly, and it needed only such a movement to tip it over. The road was strewn with hay as the three vehicles and the many horses tried to avoid each other.

Robin jumped down and ran to his horses and led them off the road. The passengers came out of the coach, demanding to know what was happening and insisting that the coach continue on its way. The farmer was only concerned with his precious load of hay, which was now scattered all over the roadway. Everyone was demanding something, but no one else could hear what it was.

Robin turned back to make sure Kitty was all right. He then realized that in the midst of the confusion she had climbed down, untied her horse, and could now be seen walking quickly down a narrow path on the other side of the road.

Any thought of following her was soon abandoned when people began to crowd around him, asking what should be done. It would take hours to unravel this problem.

"Damnation!" he whispered to himself.

CHAPTER FIVE

Mavis Tolbert was bored. She and her brother William had been sharing the same carriage now for several hours, and barely a dozen words had been exchanged. After Mavis had exhausted the topic of how each of the children was, William retreated behind his newspaper, leaving Mavis to stare out the window. This was usually the worst part of the journey, having to endure William's company for several hours, although he would have been astonished to learn it. Since Mavis never opposed him, in fact, rarely even ventured an opinion, he never considered her feelings. If he thought of her at all, he would assume that he was providing a bright spot in her otherwise empty life by letting her visit his home.

Mavis was a plain woman of medium height, with a pale complexion and pale brown hair. She was the youngest of William's brothers and sisters by several years, but instead of being lavishly petted and spoiled by the older children, she had been ignored most of the time. As a child she had done almost anything to gain their approval, and still did, even sending away the man who loved her. (They had not disapproved of Michael because they had felt he wouldn't make Mavis happy, but rather because his father was a tenant farmer. For children whose mother was not accepted by the local gentry, they were remarkably snobbish.) So Mavis sent Michael away, eventually forgot him, and convinced herself that she was well suited to her role of spinster aunt. She visited her nieces and nephews a few times a year, usually when their parents wished to be somewhere else and needed an adult to take care of them. She told herself that she really enjoyed seeing them, which did not explain why she chose to leave them very much to the care of their nurses and governesses. She knew the reason they were glad to see her was probably because her arrival meant the departure of their parents.

William's children were more tolerable, though, Mavis had to admit. Maybe it was because he did not inflict his presence on them constantly. Whatever the reason, she did tend to look forward to seeing his children more than the others.

Mavis brushed some dust from her skirt. This trip seemed even more tedious than the other ones to William's home. Although his carriage was old, it normally gave a fairly comfortable ride. Today, however, she felt considerably tossed about.

"William . . ." she ventured.

He peered around the edge of his paper and glared at her.

"Is there something wrong with one of your horses? They don't seem to be pulling evenly."

"Nonsense," he said, and went back to his paper.

Mavis settled back as well as she could and held on to a strap to keep herself from falling on the floor. She was not disturbed that William had not paid much attention to her. She had learned that few people were interested in her observations, so she usually kept them to herself. But when the carriage jolted suddenly and swerved off the road, she wasn't surprised.

William, after giving her a disgusted look, climbed out onto the road. Mavis decided to leave the coach also, as it was rather precariously tilted at the edge of the road. When she was safely out, she saw William arguing with the driver, while a groom was trying to calm the horses. Some strips of the harness lay on the ground under the carriage.

Looking around her, Mavis decided that they

were likely to be stranded there for quite a time. They could not have been more than a few miles from Crofton, but there were no houses in sight. She guessed that William would send one of his men into town to hire a carriage to take them the rest of the way. She moved off the dusty road into some shade. After a few minutes, William came over to where she was standing.

"Damned trace broke," he told her. "That fool of a driver should have known something was wrong."

He turned to glare at that unfortunate individual, who was now engaged in unhitching the horses.

"They were hitched improperly. One of the horses is lame now because of it. I can't understand how that driver couldn't tell that something was wrong."

Mavis just smiled sympathetically at him and began to brush some of the dust off her dress. William watched her for a few minutes, then turned away. He had never seen clothes as ugly as those Mavis wore. He had hoped that she could help Kitty choose some clothes for her trousseau, but he had forgotten how abominably she dressed herself. It looked as though he would have to depend on the dressmaker's help. He went back to the carriage to get his newspaper.

Mavis continued to try to clean herself off. She felt so untidy after traveling any distance, but her dress did not show the dirt much—it was a pale gray broadcloth and very sturdy. Like all her clothes, it was comfortable and extremely out of fashion.

William was wrong, though, in assuming that she did not have good taste. She knew exactly what styles were correct and what would be becoming. Her small income did not allow her to apply this knowledge to herself, so rather than wear clothes that were a few years out of fashion, she preferred to wear totally serviceable ones, which had never been in fashion.

About half an hour after the groom had started walking to town (William would not let him use the other horse), William moved away from the side of the coach where he had been leaning while reading his paper. He rummaged around inside it for a few minutes and pulled out a dusty-looking rug.

He came over to Mavis, explaining that they might as well sit down and be comfortable. He started to spread the rug on the ground when the sound of approaching horses made him stop. Tossing the rug to Mavis, he went quickly to the side of his carriage, ready to flag down the animals. Around a bend in the road came a carriage. The driver saw William's vehicle at the side of the road and slowed down and stopped.

"Do you need some assistance?" a male voice inquired.

William peered into the dimness inside the carriage. He didn't like talking to people he couldn't see clearly and was about to demand that the man get out into the open. Mavis knew that William was likely to forget that they needed help and might offend their would-be rescuer, so she stepped forward, still holding the rug.

Clutching William's arm, she said, "Perhaps this man might be willing to help us."

William remembered his present problem and took on a more humble attitude, which meant that he was only slightly less belligerent. But the carriage did not pull away and leave them there.

William explained that their carriage had met with a slight accident and that his groom had gone to Crofton to get help. When the gentleman offered to take the two of them into the town himself, William gratefully agreed. Several hours' wait along a dusty road did not appeal to him.

The carriage door opened and the gentleman stepped out. He was tall and handsome, with streaks of gray in his dark hair. He was dressed in the fashion of the day and did not look as though spending the day in a carriage bothered him at all. Mavis felt even grubbier when she saw how immaculate he looked.

"I am Sir Julian Merriot," he said, extending his hand.

"William Tolbert," William replied, shaking hands briefly. He turned toward their carriage. "Do you have room for some of our things?"

"Certainly," said Sir Julian.

"What are you still holding that stupid rug for, Mavis? Put it down, will you, and make sure that we don't leave something behind." William stomped off to the carriage and began to search for the things he wanted to bring with them.

Mavis looked at Sir Julian. He was watching her with a slight smile on his face. "I am Mavis Tolbert," she said. "It's very kind of you to give us a ride into town. I'm afraid the thought of waiting here any longer was not very agreeable."

"It's my pleasure," he said, glancing down at her left hand. "I am glad I can be of service, Miss Tolbert."

Mavis went over to help William, who had called her a few times already and looked as if the next call would be quite loud and rude.

Sir Julian watched them amusedly. It was really a stroke of luck to come upon them this way. He had lost several valuable days in London, trying to reassure his creditors, and was afraid that the wealthy Miss Tolbert might have been surrounded by admirers by this time. It seemed, however, that she was just arriving also. The problem of getting an introduction was solved too. Sir Julian took it as an omen that his luck had changed at last.

Sir Julian's groom helped with William's and Mavis's bags, and they were all loaded into the carriage. William settled himself into the space next to Sir Julian, so Mavis had to sit in the smaller seat in front of them. She watched in amusement as William struggled with himself to make polite conversation.

"You visiting around here?" William asked as the carriage started down the road.

"I'm staying at the Winfields', some cousins of mine. Perhaps you know them." One of the problems Sir Julian had faced in the last few days was to discover someone in the area whom he could visit. He finally decided on the Winfields, some distant cousins of his mother. They had extended him many invitations in the past, but he had not been anxious to recognize the connection. Mr. Winfield was a rather radical proponent of education for the masses. He had several unfashionable schools that he helped support, and his second son was actually a mathematics instructor at one of them.

But they were too conveniently placed to be ignored now. Julian could visit them and safely stay in the area as long as he wished without attracting attention. His hopes for success with this heiress were based on keeping his reputation as a fortune hunter a secret. Their meeting must appear to be a chance one.

"The Winfields live just down the road from us," Mavis told him.

"Well, perhaps I may be seeing you again soon." Sir Julian smiled at them.

"Maybe," William admitted. He was not sure who this man was who came along to help them so conveniently. Not that he had anything to do with the accident, but William was careful not to encourage the wrong sort. Of course, he did have a title, so he ought to be all right, but he wasn't accepting any invitations from Sir Julian until he did some checking on his own. He might have made up his title, for all William knew.

To Mavis's relief, Sir Julian did not seem to take offense at William's rudeness. He seemed instead to be amused by it. Soon William gave up trying to converse and began to read his paper again. Mavis thought that either he was a very slow reader or he liked to memorize the news. She thought of asking him which one it was, but because she knew he was really hiding behind it so he wouldn't have to talk, she decided to skip it. She had been watching the passing countryside for a few minutes when she realized that Sir Julian had spoken to her.

"Are you just coming from London yourself?" he asked.

"I've been there for several days," she said. "Although I have a home in Bath, I spend a good deal of time in Crofton."

"I spent some time in Bath earlier this year," he told her. "It's a town I always enjoy visiting." They began to talk about that town and some of the places in it familiar to both of them. They even discovered a few mutual acquaintances. Mavis was very surprised when they pulled into Crofton. The time had gone by very quickly.

The carriage pulled up in front of the Wild Boar, the largest inn in Crofton. William put down his newspaper and said everything proper to thank Sir Julian. Then the three of them climbed out of the coach. William's groom, whom they had picked up along the way, unloaded the Tolberts' bags from the carriage and carried them into the inn where they would wait while another carriage was prepared for them.

"Well, thank you again," said William, shaking Sir Julian's hand. "Have a pleasant stay down here." It didn't sound as though William was planning on seeing much of him. He turned and went into the inn.

Sir Julian turned to Mavis, who was watching her brother walk away. "I do hope to see you again while I'm here. I would like to call on you soon, if I might."

"Of course," Mavis assured him. "We would be happy to see you anytime you wish to call. You have been very kind in helping us, and we would consider it a privilege to repay you, in a small way, by extending our hospitality to you." She held out her hand. "Thank you again, Sir Julian."

"It was truly my pleasure, Miss Tolbert," he said.

Mavis smiled at him as he climbed into his coach, and she watched while it pulled away. William's groom had the last of the bags.

"In here, Miss Tolbert," he called to her.

She followed him through the door, where she almost collided with a tall, red-haired man, who had chosen to stop in the doorway. After begging her pardon, he stepped aside and she went in.

William was arguing with the innkeeper over the price of a carriage to take them to Crofton Grange. Finally the price was agreed on, and the man scurried away to get the carriage ready. William saw Mavis and indicated a private parlor where they could wait.

"Tried to rob me just because I needed one of his carriages. He must have thought I was a real fool if he thought I would agree to the first price he named. It was outrageous. Got him to come way down, though." William was satisfied with the results of his bargaining. He opened up his inevitable newspaper, but after one glance he closed it and threw it on the table next to him.

"It shouldn't be a long wait," he told his sister.

Mavis was quite sure that the innkeeper raised his prices considerably when he saw William coming, so he could then lower them down to his normal price, and she said nothing to William about his bargaining success. Instead, she asked how badly the carriage was damaged.

Before he could answer, the door of the parlor opened and the innkeeper came in. The carriage was waiting outside, if they would like to get on their way.

The parlor they were in opened onto the public room of the inn, where a crowd of men was consuming the cold ale that the inn boasted was the best for miles around. Usually late in the afternoon was a rather slow time at the Wild Boar, but today was an exception. There had been a cockfight about three miles away, and because Crofton was on the way back to London, many of the young men had chosen to stop there, rather than at a smaller inn along the way.

The serving girl was being harassed on all sides and could barely keep up with the orders. Rosie was a tall, friendly girl, richly endowed by nature, and was used to discouraging unwanted advances. She was merely amused at the attempts at romance made by some of the slightly foxed customers.

As William and Mavis left their parlor, some more young men were entering the inn. Mavis could not imagine where they would all sit but was not inclined to wait around to see. She prodded William, who was rather openly ogling Rosie as she maneuvered a heavily laden tray through the crowded tables. As she passed one table, a very drunken young man jumped up and blocked her way. He began an impassioned speech recounting all her charms and declaring his undying love for her. At the end of his speech he tried to grab her for a kiss, but she ducked down and slipped by him, and his kiss landed on the cheek of a portly man waiting to get by.

It was hard to decide who was more upset—the boy or the gentleman he mistakenly kissed. The rest of the room was roaring with laughter at their expense.

William joined in the laughter, too, much to Mavis's disgust. Drunken horseplay was not amusing to her. She poked William again.

"Do you think we could leave?" she asked in a rather disapproving manner.

William frowned at her. "You're such a prude. Can't even enjoy a little joke. I can see why you're still not married." He looked back at the room, which was still suffering the effects of the kiss. He started to laugh again, but this time it was more quietly.

"Good day, Mr. Tolbert, Miss Tolbert," the innkeeper called to them. "Come again soon."

Their carriage was waiting in the courtyard, with their luggage all piled on. They got in and started on their way, once more. They did not notice that two of the gentlemen from the public room were staring after them.

After Kitty had left, Robin managed to untangle the disagreement over whose fault the accident was. Eventually all the parties were satisfied and continued on their way. Robin was free to go, also, but he had little desire for it.

His original plan had been to see Scotney Park, come back to the area for the cockfight, then send a letter to William Tolbert telling him he was in Crofton and asking if he could call the next day. He had not set up a definite time for his visit because he wasn't sure how long he would be at Scotney Park.

Conditions at his estate were even worse than he had thought possible. Repairs were needed everywhere, and the farms were not producing as they should. Of course, there had been no one in residence for several years now, and the agent wasn't very competent.

The house was in disrepair also. An elderly couple was living there, but they didn't have the help needed to keep it up. A few rooms were livable, but just barely. It was definitely not a house of fashion, with the drapes rotting away at the windows and damp spots on the walls. The paintings were so dirty that many of them were impossible to identify. It had never been a major showplace, but it was, at one time, a fairly comfortable home.

Finally, he had left in despair and hoped to be cheered up when he met his friends at the cockfight. But that hadn't helped because he had met Kitty again, and he had regretted even more bitterly that he was bound by the contract his father had signed. Now Kitty was off someplace, and he still didn't know where to find her, even if he did know her name. Also he had left the cockfight so abruptly that his friends would go back to London and he would not even have their company to cheer him up.

Once he reached Crofton, Robin went to the Wild Boar. He got a room and changed his clothes, wishing he could take off his problems as easily as he could take off a soiled shirt. After losing some minutes in a brown study, he decided to take a walk around the town.

He walked to the outskirts of town before he turned back. He told himself a walk might clear his depression, but a great deal of time was spent trying to find a house belonging to the Conallys. When he had to admit failure, he reminded himself that Kitty had left several miles before they actually reached the town, so she might not live in the town itself. But it was getting too late to start wandering around the countryside in search of a house that he had no business visiting anyway.

Robin walked back to the inn mentally composing his letter to William Tolbert. If he sent it tonight, he could probably visit them tomorrow. After all, he had written them from London, so they were expecting him some time this week.

Soon he was back at the inn, but he had not progressed far in the letter. His whole mind was rebelling against the idea of the marriage, and even the slightest thing was enough to distract him from what he was trying to do. By the time he reached the public room, he was ready for some ale. Maybe the letter would come easier after he relaxed a little.

Robin was about to order his ale when he was hailed from the doorway.

"Robin! Over here, Robin!"

Robin looked over and saw Trilby behind a crowd that had just come in. When he could finally get by, he came over to where Robin was sitting.

"I hoped I'd find you here. Where'd you run off to?" Trilby looked around him. "Where's the boy?"

"Who?" Robin asked.

"The boy, Kit. The one you brought to the cockfight. You take him home?"

Robin had forgotten that the others had not known the truth about Kitty. "Yes, he went home. How did you manage to come here? Are the others with you?"

"No, they went on back. Tom had plans for later

this evening, and Peter's due at school soon, so he thought he'd better drop in to see his father for a day or two. I figured you'd be staying around here somewhere, so I was going to try all the inns 'til I caught up with you. It would have helped if you had given me a clue as to where you were going when you jumped up and left. Why'd you disappear like that anyway?" Trilby paused as he settled himself more comfortably in his chair.

"Oh, Lord," he said, jumping up. "I left my horses out there. I only meant to pop in and see if you were here. Don't give up my chair, old boy. I'll be right back." He got up and went quickly to the door, almost knocking down some people coming in.

Robin took a long drink of ale. He was lucky Trilby had not pursued that last question. Robin had not wanted to tell anybody about Kitty. He hoped Trilby would be onto some other topic by the time he returned.

Trilby was back in a few minutes. Robin had planned to distract him by telling him about the problems at Scotney Park. If you weren't involved, some of them could be really funny. But when Trilby returned he was in no mood for jokes.

"I've seen her, Robin," he said, sinking into his chair.

"Seen who?" Surely he had not seen Kitty and recognized her.

"I've seen your Miss Tolbert," he said in a whisper. "I almost knocked her down when I was going out."

"Oh, Lord," said Robin. "Is it bad?" Trilby was so still. He seemed almost to be in shock.

"Let's get out of here," Trilby suggested, "and I'll tell you about her. Someone might overhear us here."

They both got up and made their way across the room to the door. They were almost there when the door from a private parlor opened and a man and woman came out. Trilby's look clearly said that this was she. Because the two people were blocking the way, he and Trilby stayed to the side, hoping to follow them out. It was at this moment that the young man decided to proclaim his love for Rosie. Robin and Trilby were close enough to see the disgust on Miss Tolbert's face. They heard Mr. Tolbert call her a prude and comment on her lack of a husband. Robin couldn't move when they had left.

"Do you think we're wrong?" he asked Trilby.

At that time, the innkeeper, who had been way-laid by a complaining customer, called after the departing figures, "Good day, Mr. Tolbert. Miss Tolbert. Come again soon."

"I don't think we're wrong," Trilby said.

The two of them went out the door slowly. The Tolberts' carriage was pulling into the road and was soon out of sight.

"I don't think I ever really believed any of this would actually happen. Until now, that is," Robin said. He was silent for a few minutes, then looked at Trilby. "How did you know who she was?"

"I heard someone call her by name," Trilby

said. "A groom, I think." He had been too late to see Sir Julian with her.

They started walking down the street. People and horses were passing them, but they didn't notice.

"She looked older than I expected," Robin finally said. In his mind he kept comparing Kitty's youthful face and figure to the more mature Miss Tolbert.

"Of course," Robin admitted, "she may be a really pleasant person. You can't go by the way she looks."

"That's true," Trilby agreed, hoping to cheer him up. "Wait 'til you meet her. Her clothes aren't up to snuff, but you could change all that. Maybe transform her into a real beauty."

"Sure," said Robin, "except she must be ten years older than I am, and her own father called her a prude. That's a high recommendation."

"I think you ought to go back to Scotney Park for a few days," Trilby advised. "Merriot should be around here soon. Give him a few days to work before you show up. If you're a few days late, it'll only make them dislike you."

"That's a good idea," Robin agreed. He looked at his watch. "If I left soon, I should be able to reach the park before sundown."

"Don't give up," Trilby smiled at him. "I'm sure everything's going to work out fine."

Robin nodded, but he didn't really believe his friend's optimistic forecast.

CHAPTER SIX

"We don't have much time left," William was saying after dinner that night. "I expect Lord Scotney at any time, and there's still a lot to be done. Tomorrow you'll have to go into town and see Mrs. Fantley. She makes the clothes for a lot of the women around here, so she'll know what is in style. Ask her to arrange for a hairdresser to come here tomorrow afternoon. She'll know where to find one."

Mavis looked nervously at Kitty. She had not had any time to talk to her niece since her arrival that afternoon, but Kitty certainly did not look like a girl who was approaching her wedding with any enthusiasm. Maybe before Kitty went to bed, she would have a chance to talk to her.

Finally William finished with his orders and sent them off to their rooms, saying they would have a long day tomorrow.

Kitty was almost ready for bed when Nellie came into her room. Most of the things they were going to buy the next day were for Kitty, but the other girls were getting a few things also.

"I've almost decided on yellow muslin for mine," Nellie said as she bounced onto Kitty's bed.

"Your what?" asked Kitty, staring out of the window into the darkened garden below. The night was warm, and the fragrance of roses came in through the open casement.

"My new dress, silly," Nellie answered. "With long ribbons hanging down from the waist. Kitty, do stop looking out the window and pay attention. You're awfully quiet tonight. What did you and Letty do today? You've been so gloomy since you came home."

Kitty was about to tell Nellie that she hadn't seen Letty all day, when she remembered that she was supposed to have spent the day there. "Oh, nothing much," Kitty said as she took off her dressing gown. "If you must sit on the bed, at least do it at the other end, so I can get in."

She sat down with her legs under the covers and faced Nellie.

"Why have you picked yellow muslin before you even see what there is to choose from? You already have a whole closet full of yellow. Can't you think of any other color?"

Nellie got up and put Kitty's wrap around her. She was almost the same height as her older sister, although she probably would be taller than she eventually. She went over to the mirror and began to pose in front of it, holding her hair up in elaborate styles.

"I think I look older in yellow," she said.

"You look like you're about ten like that," Kitty

laughed, ducking the pillow that Nellie threw at her.

"What colors are you going to choose, since you're so full of advice tonight?" Nellie asked, climbing back on the bed.

"Black, I think," said Kitty. "I'm going into mourning for my future."

"Oh, don't go all gloomy again or I'll leave," Nellie threatened. "Alicia's description of fashionable marriages probably is something she made up. Or even if some people feel like that I doubt that very many do. You don't even know what Lord Scotney is like. He might be very nice. He might be young and handsome and will fall madly in love with you the first time that he sees you."

"No, Alicia's right," Kitty said. "Even the people you really admire think marriage is something separate from love. You marry one person while you love someone else."

Kitty got up and began to brush her hair, finding relief in the hard, fast strokes. A knock at her door stopped her. Their aunt opened the door and looked in.

"Oh, I thought you'd be alone, Kitty," she said.

"I'll go if you wanted to talk privately," Nellie offered.

"Oh, no," said Mavis. "I didn't mean for you to go." It was true that she had wanted to talk to Kitty in private, but it seemed rude to practically demand that someone leave a room to suit her convenience.

"I was just wondering how you were, that's all," she said.

"Well, we're happy that you came by," said Nellie, ignoring her sister's questioning look. "Why don't you sit down? . . . Unless you're too tired to talk awhile," she added.

"Oh, I'm not tired," said Mavis, closing the door after her. "Do you really want me to stay and talk?"

"Of course we do," Nellie insisted.

"It's been a long time since we've had a good talk," Kitty added.

Mavis could have told her that they had never had a good talk, but she was too curious as to why she had suddenly been invited in.

"Have you ever been in love?" Nellie asked abruptly.

Mavis got panicky for a moment. That old affair with Michael was never brought up as far as she knew. How could these girls have heard about it? If they hadn't heard about it, why were they asking her about love? She knew of no one who would consider her an expert on the subject. Alicia probably knew more about it than she did.

"Why do you ask?" she finally managed to say. Surely they weren't going to embarrass her or, worse still, laugh at her because of it.

"We were having an argument," Nellie explained, "about something that Alicia told us."

"And we thought you might be able to help," Kitty finished for her.

Mavis looked at the two girls. She was truly fond of them and didn't think that they were the type to make fun of her. She didn't know if she could trust them not to tell the others about Michael if she confided in them. No one had ever asked her for advice before, and she felt she had a certain responsibility to answer their questions. Could she shrug it off merely because she was afraid that they might ridicule her?

"Yes," she told them, "I was in love once."

Nellie was surprised. She had asked her aunt because she thought Mavis might know more of the ways of polite society than Alicia, but she had never expected to learn that she had been in love.

"Who was he?" Kitty asked, curling up on her pillows.

Mavis walked over to the bed and sat down on the end, near Nellie. It didn't seem quite so hard once she started.

"His name was Michael, and he was in the navy."

"Where did you meet him?" Nellie wanted to know.

"We met in London when he was stationed there for a brief time. He was terribly handsome, or I thought so. He hated the city and wanted to spend his free time in the parks. He used to say that it was as close as he could come to being back home in the country. Then he received word that he was to go and meet his ship. We only had a few weeks together."

"Why didn't you get married?" Nellie asked. "Was he killed?" In Nellie's mind there always had to be an awfully good reason keeping lovers apart.

Mavis stopped for a minute. She felt her answer to that question was important. If she made it seem as though she was sorry later that she refused him, the girls might want to disregard their father's wishes when they were to be married. She looked at Kitty's drawn face and wondered if that wasn't the base of the problem that she had sensed since her arrival. But to stick only to the fact that Michael was beneath her socially would disregard her feelings and her doubts. Was it really honest to ignore them?

"No, he was not killed. There was really no question of our getting married."

Both Kitty and Nellie stared at her. Obviously she was not going to get by with such a simple explanation.

"His father was a tenant farmer," she said, as if this clarified everything.

There was still no response from either girl.

"He was beneath me socially," she told them.

They still looked at her in expectation, thinking there had to be more of a reason.

Mavis had never felt so uncomfortable in all her life. They were not at all shocked that she had fallen in love with the son of a tenant farmer, as she had expected them to be. She had the feeling that they were going to be more upset by the fact that she had allowed her family to make her decision for her. She watched them nervously as they watched her back. In what way was William raising his children? Didn't he instill in them the proper respect for social restrictions? She was feeling more doubts, now, about the wisdom of her decision than she had eleven years ago, when it had been made.

"My family forbade the marriage," she whispered, "because he was beneath me."

Suddenly Mavis found herself crying. She wasn't sure why, but the tears were streaming down her face, and she didn't seem able to stop them. Kitty came over and put her arms around her. It was meant to be a comforting gesture, but it only made her cry all the more.

After a few minutes in which she allowed herself the luxury of crying her heart out, Mavis realized what a terrible example she was setting for her young nieces. She managed to stop crying and, while mopping her eyes with a handkerchief that Nellie had found for her, she smiled wetly at them.

"I'm sorry," she said. "I'm not sure what got into me."

"We understood, didn't we, Kitty?" Nellie said. "You really loved him a lot, didn't you? But how could you let your family stand in your way?"

"No, I don't think I really did love him," Mavis said. "I think it was because he was nice and not frightening like some of the other men I had met. I certainly liked him a lot, but I don't think I loved him. If I really had, would I have stopped thinking about him years ago?"

"But if you didn't love him, why did you need your family to make your decision for you? Couldn't you have decided yourself?" Kitty asked.

Mavis blew her nose defiantly. "I'm not very good at arguing or sticking to my wishes against opposition. Michael was sure that I loved him, but I wasn't. It seemed easier to rely on the guidelines that I had always followed. We were from different worlds socially, and I had always been taught that I was superior to farmers and people in trade."

She could see a question in their eyes.

"Yes, even my mother, whose own father was in trade, felt that way. She was the one who preached it most strongly. She felt that our father's blood predominated over hers and that we were part of the socially elite, even if no one else but us recognized the fact. If I had married Michael, I would not have been welcomed by my family again."

"I don't think they . . ." Nellie stopped.

"I know. They don't really welcome me now, but they were my whole world at that time. Now I wonder if it would have been better to marry Michael without love and try to make him happy. But I'll never know."

She straightened up and smiled at them. "This certainly isn't what I had come in here to talk about. I had hoped Kitty and I could discuss her wedding."

"Could we wait until tomorrow to talk about it?" Kitty asked.

"Certainly," said Mavis, glancing at Nellie.

"Oh, it's not because Nellie is here," Kitty said. "She knows my feelings about it, but I'd just rather wait." Mavis's story was upsetting, and though it seemed to Kitty to back up her side, she hesitated to make use of it while Mavis was still so emotional.

"I understand," Mavis said, and really did. She stood up. "Good night, girls. Sleep well."

Kitty ran over and hugged her aunt. "Good night, Aunt Mavis. Thank you for telling us." She kissed her on the cheek.

Mavis smiled rather self-consciously and went out quickly.

Nellie looked at Kitty. "She's nice," Nellie said. "She looks so dowdy on the outside, but she's really very nice inside."

"Yes, she is," Kitty agreed, "and she must have looked more attractive when she met Michael. If we could get her to dress more fashionably, she might find someone else."

"Maybe we could marry her off to Lord Scotney," Nellie suggested.

"Oh, no," said Kitty, in disgust. "She deserves somebody much better than him."

The next morning, Mavis, Kitty, Alicia, and Nellie were all whisked off to the dressmakers before Mavis had a chance to talk privately with Kitty. She was afraid that she had left the girls with the wrong impression the night before but she decided not to worry about it.

After the girls had chosen their dresses, Mavis ordered one for herself. She quickly picked out a lavender muslin, but Kitty and Nellie were appalled and managed to talk her into some gold material that they had found. Mavis finally agreed to it for a morning dress and let an assistant take her measurements. While she was occupied, the girls asked Mrs. Fantley to make up an evening dress for her also, assuring her that their father would pay for it. She agreed, saying she had a gray material that would be perfect. Kitty and Nellie wanted anything but gray, but as Mavis had rejoined them, they had to trust the dressmaker.

They finished their shopping and were back at Crofton Grange for a late lunch.

William was pleased with the excitement over their purchases. If Kitty was taking more of an interest in her clothes, perhaps she was starting to accept her marriage. He didn't even protest when the girls told him he was paying for Mavis's new dress. His only concern was that they remembered to arrange a visit from the hairdresser.

After lunch, Mavis was determined to have her talk with Kitty, so she set off to look for her. She finally found her sorting a box of ribbons in her bedroom.

"I thought it was time that we had our talk," Mavis said as she closed the door. "You don't seem to be altogether pleased with the marriage that your father has arranged for you. He has your best interests in mind, you know. Why do you object to it so?"

"He doesn't have my best interests in mind," Kitty told her. "All he wants is for us to have a title in the family. He doesn't even know the man I'm supposed to marry."

"Of course he knows him," Mavis insisted. "Why

I met him myself, when the contract was signed. Claude came down himself. He'll make you a fine husband."

"But I'm not marrying Claude," said Kitty. "Claude died last year, and now I'm to marry his younger brother. I don't even know his nâme. Father knows nothing about him except that he's got the title, and that's all that counts with him. He has no way of knowing what kind of person the new Earl is, but he won't reconsider."

"Well, I didn't know about Claude," said Mavis, sitting down on the edge of the bed. "It does seem rather hard to marry someone you haven't met."

"I knew you'd understand." Kitty sighed in relief as she sat down next to her aunt. "After what you told us last night, I was sure you wouldn't think I should marry someone just because my father wants me to. I knew I could count on your support."

Mavis got up and walked slowly around the room. "But you don't have my support, Kitty. I think you have to follow your father's wishes. You have to trust that he knows best for you."

"How can you say that, after all you went through?" Kitty cried. "Do you want my life dictated by others like yours was?"

"But you aren't in any position to know what's best for you, any more than I was. Once Michael left, I got over him very quickly. I think we were both just lonely. It's true that I've wondered what my life would have been like had I married him, but I think that any unmarried woman dreams about someone she might have married. I think my family was right in the long run. There were problems that we might have encountered that I know nothing about. It is easy to dream how nice it might be to be loved and cherished and never lonely, but I don't think Michael was the answer for me."

"You're just saying that now because you want me to go along with Father's wishes," Kitty accused.

"No, Kitty," Mavis said. "I'm saying it because I really believe that you must be guided by your father's plans."

"Well, I won't." Kitty jumped up from the bed and ran to the door. "I'm not going to marry him. I'll never believe that everybody else but me has the right to order my life about." She ran out of the room, slamming the door behind her.

CHAPTER SEVEN

After Kitty had left her room, Mavis sank down on the chair near Kitty's dressing table. She had been hopeful this morning that she might influence the girls toward more responsible behavior. Now Kitty thought very badly of her. Kitty felt that Mavis had obeyed her family with disastrous results, yet Mavis was now encouraging Kitty to do the same.

Mavis picked up a ribbon that Kitty had dropped on the floor, remembering how, when she was a child, she could hardly wait until she grew up so that her life would be simple and uncomplicated. She wondered now if her life was ever due to be simple and uncomplicated.

"Miss Tolbert?" a voice from the doorway asked.

"Yes," she answered absently. She was staring off into space, twisting the ribbon around her fingers.

"Ah," the voice said, coming closer. "This will be a challenge."

Suddenly Mavis felt someone pulling the pins out of her hair. Half of it was falling down her back when she turned around. A short, dark-haired man was standing behind her. He was holding a comb and had a selection of scissors with him. A maid stood at the open door.

"Who are you?" Mavis demanded.

"I am Marlin," he said, in a voice just as haughty as hers. "I am here to cut your hair. I was told you were a young girl, but you look more like an old maid of forty."

"I am only thirty," said Mavis angrily. "And you are not here to cut my hair, but my niece's."

Marlin bowed slightly, as a concession to his error, and turned to leave. Mavis peered into the mirror in front of her as she tried to pin her hair up once more.

"Do I really look like I'm forty?" she asked him.

He shrugged. "Maybe only thirty-eight." He walked back to her. "You make it too sober. Hair must be loose, to make a frame for your face." He took over fixing her hair. Although he pinned it up much as Mavis did, it was looser and the effect was very different.

"Age makes the face more severe, the lines of the bones are harsher. The hair must add the softness a woman's face needs for beauty." It did look better the way he held it. "It has good color," he said, indicating her hair, "but it is too heavy. I will trim it for you."

Mavis stared dumbly into the mirror, still shocked by the fact that he had said she looked more like forty than thirty. She wasn't really aware that she had consented until she felt him pulling his comb through her thick hair. He put a cover over her dress and was suddenly cutting and trimming. Mavis felt a moment of panic. What was he doing to her hair? She could see herself with a mutilated head of hair, too short to even try to hide it by pinning it up in a plain style. She tried to stop him, but he ignored her. Why can't I just stand up for myself? she asked herself. She heard movement behind her and saw, in the corner of the mirror, that Kitty had come back in the room. From the redness of her eyes, Mavis guessed how she had spent the last half hour. Kitty seemed to be too amazed by the happenings in the room to speak. Finally she came over to Mavis.

"Is he the hairdresser?" she asked quietly.

"I certainly hope so," Mavis answered.

Kitty watched for a few minutes. "Aunt Mavis . . ." she began.

"Not now, child," said Mavis. She held out her hand and smiled at Kitty as well as she could without moving her head. Kitty smiled back weakly and squeezed her hand.

"If you please," said Marlin. He was trying to get around Mavis and did not approve of people being distracted while he fixed their hair.

Mavis meekly withdrew her hand, and he continued working. Kitty sat on the edge of the bed to watch. She started to ask a question but received such a fierce look from Marlin that she retreated into silence.

In a surprisingly short time, quite a pile of Mavis's hair lay on the floor. The maid started to sweep it up, while Marlin pinned up what was left.

"It will be a simple style. Becoming, yet not the height of fashion." He peered rudely at her dress. "You do not want, I think, the height of fashion."

Mavis agreed, rather put out by his assumption. She was wishing her new dress had been finished, then he would not assume that she was some dowdy old spinster.

"You see," Marlin was saying. "Simple, but elegant."

Mavis looked into the mirror. It was nice, not really that different from her old style, but fuller and softer. She looked almost attractive.

"It's beautiful, Aunt Mavis," Kitty said after

Marlin had nodded to her, indicating that she was allowed to speak now. "Nobody will recognize you."

Mavis wasn't sure that that was a compliment, but she let it slip by because Marlin was shooing her out of the chair. The maid came over and brushed off the stray hairs that had managed to fall on her gown. Kitty had already taken her place in front of Marlin.

"What has happened to your hair?" he asked as he unpinned the back. "It looks like you cut it yourself. It will take some work, I fear."

He started cutting and combing Kitty's hair, muttering to himself as he worked. Mavis hid a smile as she slipped out of the room. Alicia should approve of him, anyway. He felt that good hair and style were very important. She went down the hall, looking in various rooms until she found Alicia, and sent her to Kitty's room to wait her turn.

Everyone slept late the next morning and woke to find the sun shining. Kitty and Alicia went out for a long ride after breakfast, while Nellie went in search of Willy and Tim, and William rode off to inspect some of his farms with his agent. Mavis found herself all alone by the middle of the morning. She had just sat down to write some letters when a groom came to tell her that some packages had arrived from Mrs. Fantley.

Mavis put down her pen and went to the hall to sort out the delivery. There were the shawls, ribbons, and undergarments that the girls had chosen, and surprisingly enough, her gold dress had been completed and was there.

After the groom took the boxes up to the girls' rooms, Mavis took her own dress upstairs. She was anxious to see how it would look on her. She pulled it out from the wrappings. The style was very simple. The skirt flowed gently out from a tight, high waistband. Because the fabric was so fine, the skirt had several layers. The top layer was scalloped and edged with dark brown ribbon. More ribbons hung from a small bow at the waist. The sleeves were small, with the same brown ribbon trim. Mavis felt like a young girl trying on her first evening dress.

Once she had it on, she straightened her hair, then walked over to the full-length mirror. She was almost afraid to look at herself. She had worn dowdy clothes for so long that she was afraid she would look ridiculous in something prettier.

Somehow she managed to get herself in front of the mirror with her eyes closed. Very slowly, she opened them. She thought she actually looked pretty! She had never been a pretty woman; even as a girl, when she had had her season, she had been awkward and plain. But the plain girl was gone. Not that she looked beautiful, she was quite quick to admit to herself. But she thought she looked attractive. The gold in her dress made her hair seem a darker brown, but with rich, golden highlights.

Mavis was anxious to have Kitty and Nellie see her new dress. She hoped that they would like it and not think she looked silly. She took it off carefully, wanting to save it for a special occasion, and hung it up with her other dresses.

She caught a glimpse of herself in the mirror, after she had gotten dressed again. Her gray dress looked very plain compared to her new finery. She thought for a moment, then searched through her bureau for a lace cap that she had bought in a small shop in London. It had not been too expensive, and because it was trimmed in thin gray ribbons, she had decided that it was a practical addition to her wardrobe.

She put the lace cap on, noting that it covered most of her new hairstyle. Perhaps that was just as well, because she wasn't used to the style yet.

Once the cap was in place, Mavis looked in the mirror again. She still seemed to lack color. Feeling rather reckless, she decided that she needed some jewelry. The string of pearls that she had received from her father would not be appropriate to wear in the morning, but she did have a lovely garnet brooch that would be just the thing. She pinned it on and was quite pleased with the effect.

Mavis went back downstairs to continue her letter writing, but she decided instead to walk in the gardens. William's gardens were extensive and well cared for. In order to convince herself that she was being useful, she procured a basket and some shears from the gardener and went to pick some roses.

Mavis had worked her way among the bushes along the side of the house when she heard a carriage pull up. A groom came out to take the horses around to the stables and when the visitor spoke to him, pointed in her direction. The horses disappeared around the other side of the house, and a gentleman came along the path toward her. She lost sight of him momentarily and started forward to meet him. Coming around a large lilac bush, she came face to face with Sir Julian Merriot.

"Sir Julian," Mavis said, "what a pleasant surprise. How are the Winfields? Did any of them come with you?" She looked past him but saw no one else. "I'm afraid that William is not here right now. Everyone else is out riding."

"That's convenient," he said, smiling at her, "because I came to see you." They started to walk along the path. "I don't need to ask how you are, because I can see that you are quite well. Very lovely, in fact." He smiled even more at her obvious confusion. The quiet, self-assured lady he had met a few days ago must not have had much experience with compliments, because his tended to reduce her to a state of embarrassment rather easily. Of course, if she always wore clothes as unbecoming as the dress she had on now, he didn't suppose too many gentlemen were moved to sing praises of her beauty. He closed his eyes, mentally, to her dowdiness and tried to imagine that her dress was made of the finest silk and that that hideous brooch held a huge ruby, not a garnet.

"This is a lovely garden," he said. "You look very much as if you belong here."

"That's silly," said Mavis, although she was

secretly pleased, as she had never thought of herself that way. "What would I do in a garden all day? Would you like some tea? Or a glass of wine? We could sit on the terrace if you like."

"I'd much rather walk in the gardens with you if I might. Unfortunately, I have an engagement and can't stay."

She pointed out a pleasant path, and they walked along it in silence for a few minutes. They came to a small clearing where there was a bench, and they sat down.

"The actual reason that I came," Sir Julian said, "was to find out if you were going to the assembly Sunday evening. I was hoping that you would promise me some dances."

"Oh, I don't know," Mavis said. She had never expected this. "I imagine that we will go, but I don't usually dance at these affairs."

"Why ever not?" he asked. "You must disappoint a number of gentlemen."

"I'm just so out of practice," Mavis hesitated, ignoring the rest of his comment. She couldn't admit that she had stopped dancing because she was so rarely asked. It had always seemed easier to say you weren't dancing than to make excuses for yourself as to why no one was asking you.

"Well, you have all of tomorrow to brush up on your skills. You know you can't refuse me. I know so few people in the area that I'd be left all by myself."

"How absurd," laughed Mavis. "There are any number of attractive girls who would be delighted to dance with you. Surely the Winfields will introduce you to many of the people there."

"I'm afraid they aren't going. They made other plans for the evening and I'm to be on my own. Come now, I'm at your mercy."

"Oh, all right," she agreed. "If I step all over your feet, though, you have only yourself to blame, because I gave you fair warning. But I still will introduce you to some of the young girls there."

"Not too many, please," he pleaded. "They all have an alarming tendency to giggle and simper until I want to throttle them."

"Well, I have been warned also," Mavis said. "I shall try not to do either while I'm near you. Imagine what a scene we would cause if I smashed your feet with my dancing and then giggled and simpered until you tried to choke me. I'm afraid that wouldn't do."

"Somehow, I think I'm safe from such a scene," he laughed, thinking wryly that she would not be too likely to behave in such a flirtatious manner. They got up and walked back toward the house.

"I am sorry to leave so quickly," he said. "It's much pleasanter here than in a stuffy old inn, discussing business."

"I wish you would accept some refreshments," Mavis said. "It doesn't seem right to send you away without something."

"Well, you could give me one of these roses," he said, "for my coat."

"Certainly," she agreed. "Which color would you like? The white one would look well with your brown coat, or maybe this yellow. We have some lovely gold ones. It wouldn't take me but a moment to cut one."

"No," he said, "I'd like this one." He pulled out a deep red flower from her basket. It was beautifully formed and just beginning to open. "It's just the color of your brooch. Can you put it on for me?"

Mavis took the flower with a hand that shook in the most alarming fashion. This man had a very disturbing manner. Why did he pay her such outrageous compliments?

"There," she said, when she had finished, "it looks very nice. That color goes better with your coat than the others I suggested."

"That's not why I chose it."

Was she imagining that alarming twinkle in his eye?

"I needed something to remind me of pleasanter things during my dull luncheon." He caught her hand and brought it to his lips. "I shall be looking forward to Sunday evening." He nodded slightly and hurried away.

Mavis stood staring at him for a few minutes before she realized that she had never said good-bye to him.

"Oh, good day, sir," she called after him. Goodness! Now she was shouting across the garden like some rude schoolgirl!

After breakfast, Nellie went in search of her brothers. Tim was due back at school next week, and they were probably off getting into some kind of mischief. She eventually tracked them down near the creek bed, trying to catch frogs. What they were going to do with them she didn't know, and she had no desire to ask.

"Hello," she called to them from across the creek.

Willy seemed rather embarrassed at being caught in such an unsophisticated pursuit. He was trying to melt into the background until he learned if Nellie was alone. If Alicia was there, he would never hear the end of it.

"Hi," Tim called back. "Come over and help us. I've caught two so far. Willy's got four." He proudly showed her a basket that held all six frogs, none too happily.

"There's a place that's easy to cross a little downstream," Willy told her, now that he had discovered that she was alone.

When Nellie joined them, the two boys were absorbed in the pursuit of two more of the amphibians. Only after the two that they were pursuing had escaped did they pay any more attention to their sister.

"What are you doing here?" Willy wondered. He had opened another basket near some bushes and pulled out some fruit.

"I wanted to talk to you by ourselves, and this seemed like my best chance." Tim wandered back to the creek. "Tim!" Nellie shouted. "Will you come back here and listen? This is important!"

Tim came back, but clearly wondered what

could be more important than catching frogs. He seemed slightly appeased by the food that Willy offered him, so he sat down to listen.

"It's about Kitty's wedding," Nellie began.

"Oh, no," Tim protested. "I'm not going to stay here and listen to you talk about weddings." He got up in disgust.

"Sit down," Willy ordered. "Can't you think of something besides yourself?"

Tim began to sulk, but he did sit down.

"What's the problem?" Willy asked Nellie. "I know she's unhappy about the wedding, but she doesn't really tell me much."

"Of course she's unhappy," Nellie cried. "She knows nothing about him. Not even his name."

"She does so know his name," Tim insisted, still angry that he had to listen to a lot of romantic nonsense. "He's Lord Scotney, or the Earl of Scotney. She's got two perfectly good names to choose from."

Willy gave him a dirty look, while Nellie continued. "She just doesn't want to be forced into a marriage with someone she doesn't know. Father won't listen to reason. All he thinks about is the title. We had hoped that Aunt Mavis would talk him out of it, but she won't."

"Aunt Mavis! That's a laugh!" Tim scoffed. "She always agrees with everybody."

"You shut up, Timothy Tolbert!" Nellie shouted at him. "Or I'll dump all those frogs out. This is a serious problem."

Tim got very quiet. He still did not see the

seriousness of the topic, but he dearly wanted those frogs to take back to school with him. Every one of his teachers was going to get a surprise, and he didn't have much time left to catch all he needed. He edged closer to the basket in case he was called upon to protect it.

"What can we do?" Willy asked. "Father isn't too likely to listen to Aunt Mavis, but he sure isn't going to listen to us.

"No, I never meant for us to ask him," Nellie said, "but there must be a way to stop it."

Nellie and Willy sat in silence for a few minutes. Tim was eyeing a new frog that had hopped onto the bank near him. He eased himself slightly closer to it.

"I don't know what all the fuss is about," Tim told them. They were about to accuse him of not caring about Kitty's happiness when he interrupted them. "All you have to do is eliminate Lord Scotney from the picture, then how can she marry him?" The frog took a small jump closer, watching a fly that buzzed near Tim's knee.

"Just how are we going to convince him that he shouldn't marry Kitty?" Nellie asked with disdain.

"I didn't say anything about convincing him," Tim said with exaggerated patience. "I said eliminate him."

"Make sense, Tim," Willy insisted.

"You find him first. Watch him, and then," Tim said, "you pounce." With that he threw himself down and came up with the squirming frog. He held him up proudly.

Nellie jumped up and ran for the basket of frogs. Tim saw what she was doing, but he was trying to hold on to his latest prize.

"Don't you dare!" he yelled, but he was too late. Nellie opened up the basket and the frogs started jumping out. One last one couldn't quite make it, so she turned the basket upside down and shook it so it would go free.

Tim was screaming with rage by this time. He needed those frogs, and he could never catch them all again. It had been hard enough to persuade Willy to help him in the first place.

Nellie was about to toss the basket into the creek. That was the last straw. Tim made a grab for it, but as he did so, his one last frog jumped out of his hands. He started to try to recapture it, but Nellie tripped him.

"I'm sick of your stupid frogs," she shouted at him, still holding the basket. "You can't think of anything but them. You're a horrible brother."

Tim tried to grab the basket, but she managed to keep it out of his way. Finally he jumped for it as she held it above her head, but he only succeeded in knocking her down. She fell into the mud near the edge of the creek, frightening one slow-moving frog who jumped across her to escape.

"Now look what you've done to me!" she screamed at Tim. She swung the basket at his head, hitting him hard on the right side. She started to swing it again when she heard Willy yelling at them both.

"Stop it! Stop it, both of you!"

He tried to pull Tim away, but Tim had managed to get ahold of the basket and wasn't about to let go. Nellie was standing again by this time, but she too was still holding the basket. Suddenly the handle broke and Nellie fell backwards. She slipped back a few feet in the mud, trying to regain her balance, but it was no use. She landed, with a large splash, in the middle of the creek.

The sight of her sitting there, all muddy, with her hair coming down, was too much for Tim. He started laughing and could hardly stand. The look in Nellie's eyes made Willy move swiftly. With one quick shove, Tim found himself sitting right next to Nellie in the creek. That was too much for both of them. The two started to smile, then laugh until they could hardly stop. Nellie was wiping her eyes when she spotted Willy standing on the bank, watching them, as if they were two errant children who needed to be disciplined occasionally. Nellie looked at Tim, who seemed to read her mind. The two of them jumped up, and before Willy knew what they were planning, he was in the creek too.

"That didn't solve the problem," Nellie said, trying to wring the water out of her skirt. "I promised Kitty that we'd help, and I'm no closer to any suggestions."

"I gave you one," Tim insisted. "We should find out when he's coming, pose as highwaymen, and kill him. . . . We'd have to find some pistols, though," he added, as an afterthought.

"We can't do that, Tim," Willy said. He suspected that Tim was still a little peeved because he had lost his frogs. "I think that Nellie ought to get back to the house to change."

Nellie started to protest, but Willy assured her, "I'll come with you and we can discuss things on the way. Tim can stay here if he wants to."

Nellie agreed. She thought that Willy was likely to prove more help than Tim anyway, and Tim was just distracting them.

"We'll leave you the food," Willy called to him. Tim was already in the bushes searching for his frogs. "Come on, Nellie."

The two of them walked slowly back to the house. Once they were in the sun, they both felt warmer.

"You know, I think Tim did have a point," Willy said.

"You mean kill him? I don't think Kitty would go that far to get rid of him."

"No, I mean that we have to find a way to convince Lord Scotney that he doesn't want to marry Kitty, short of killing him, though." Nellie was silent. "I wonder," Willy said thoughtfully, "do you think we could just threaten him a little?"

"Of course not," Nellie cried. "This has to be clever. You can't just say, 'Don't marry my sister, or I'll beat you up!' He'd just have to tell Father ... besides, he might be a lot bigger than you."

"That's true." Willy looked down at his sparse frame. He doubted that there were many people whom he could beat up.

"There must be some way, though, that we could convince him that Kitty is not the right wife for him," Willy thought.

"I think we'd do better to find a reason for Father to forbid the marriage. He's the one who's all for it," Nellie said. "Maybe Lord Scotney has got a dark, terrible secret in his past, and we could expose him."

"How would we find out such a dark secret? Ask him? To convince Father might be the best course, but I don't think we could do that as easily as convince Lord Scotney."

They reached the outskirts of the garden and walked through them in silence.

"I'll keep thinking," Willy reassured Nellie when he saw how downcast she was. "Between the two of us, we're bound to come up with a terrible defect in Kitty's character that will prevent her from marrying him."

They ignored the stares from a downstairs maid and went to their rooms to change. By the time that luncheon was served, all traces of the creek had vanished from their clothes.

CHAPTER EIGHT

"You should not have chosen that dress, Kitty," Alicia told her impatiently. "It's so obviously last year's style."

It was Sunday evening and they were gathered in the drawing room, waiting to go to the assembly. Alicia was getting anxious because Mavis had not yet appeared.

"She knows what time we wanted to leave," Alicia complained. "She ought to be down here. I can't see what's taking her so long anyway. It's not as though she fixes herself up a lot." She moved away from the window where she had been standing and began to pace up and down the room. "There is a limit to what you can do with a plain, ugly, gray dress."

"She's wearing her new evening dress," Nellie told them. "It came about an hour ago, and I sent it right up. I thought she might want to wear it. Maybe it didn't fit right." She didn't tell them that the only reason that the dress had come that day was because she had sent a note to Mrs. Fantley in Mavis's name. In it she had promised the dressmaker a bonus if the dress was done in time for the assembly.

William entered the room. He didn't often come to the assemblies, but he'd decided this time to escort them.

"It's finally come," he said, holding high a letter. "Was waiting for me this afternoon."

No one looked even remotely interested in his letter. Alicia was even annoyed.

"Who cares about some letter? We're going to be terribly late if we don't leave soon. . . . Kitty, your dress will be all wrinkled if you sit down. You should stay standing, like me. It would keep your dress much fresher."

"Are you going to stand in the carriage, too?" Nellie asked innocently.

Alicia glared at her and walked back to stare out the window.

"He's coming tomorrow," William told them happily.

Alicia still stared out the window, while Kitty absently played with her fan. Only Nellie was paying any attention.

"Who?" she asked.

"Lord Scotney!" William was very excited.

Kitty jumped up, dropping her fan. Alicia came away from the window, while Nellie went to the door.

"I'll go see if Aunt Mavis needs any help," Nellie said on her way out.

Alicia came over and sat down next to her father, leaning eagerly toward him.

"What does he say?" she asked. "Why is he so late in coming? Oh . . . could I read the letter?"

William was pleased with her response. He handed the letter to her. If only Kitty could see the advantages of this marriage as Alicia did. He looked around for her. She was standing by the window, looking out at the darkened garden. Well, at least she hadn't started another argument.

"Want to see the letter, too?" he asked her.

She shook her head. He shrugged his shoulders and turned back to Alicia.

"It doesn't say much," she said, and handed it back to him. "I guess I was expecting more. But"— she brightened up—"we'll finally get to see him tomorrow."

William folded the letter and put it back into his pocket. "I thought he should have apologized for the delay or at least explained it."

"Father," Alicia scolded. "He's an Earl, you know. Earls don't have to explain things like that."

William nodded. Kitty turned and gave them both a disgusted look, but neither one noticed it.

The door opened and Nellie and Mavis came in.

"Doesn't she look beautiful?" Nellie beamed. "Isn't her new dress gorgeous? Turn around, Aunt Mavis, and let them see the whole thing."

Mavis turned around as ordered. Even Alicia was speechless, and she had earlier prepared a few remarks about the rudeness of keeping people waiting.

"Its not too fussy, is it?" Mavis asked nervously.

"No," Alicia said. "I have to admit, it's very nice. Not what I had pictured a gray dress to be at all."

It was, strictly speaking, a gray dress. But when Mavis moved and the light caught it, it looked more like silver. It seemed to shimmer and gleam with a life of its own. The material was light and soft, and the style was very simple. From a high waistline, the skirt fell in soft folds around her ankles. Small flowers were embroidered along the bottom and the neckline in silver threads.

"You don't think the neck is too low?" Mavis asked. She was rather self-conscious about it and felt that she ought to cover herself up more.

"Oh, no. It's perfect the way it is," Kitty insisted.

"Now, if only there was a handsome gentleman to impress tonight," Nellie said with a sigh.

The poor light in the room hid Mavis's blush.

"Did you hear the news?" William asked her.

"Yes. Nellie told me about Lord Scotney," Mavis said. She looked over at Kitty, who was busy putting on her gloves; Mavis could not tell what she was thinking.

"We really ought to leave," Alicia reminded them.

"Oh, yes," said Mavis. Nellie helped her with her light shawl and gloves as the others went into the hall.

"Have a good time, Aunt Mavis," whispered

Nellie. She gave her aunt a quick hug. "Just remember how beautiful you look, and don't you dare hide in a corner."

Mavis smiled and followed the others out.

They were as late as Alicia had feared. The dancing had already begun, and many of the men were settled in the card room. As soon as he saw that the women were settled, William disappeared, looking for some of his friends and for something stronger to drink than the lemonade served to the ladies.

Alicia and Kitty were asked to dance very quickly. Mavis talked to a few people, but all the while she was searching the room and watching the door.

This is silly, she told herself. I'm going to have a good time and not just wait around to see if he comes. She did not have to ask herself who "he" was.

When she was asked to dance she did so, and was soon having an enjoyable time. At the end of one dance, when her escort had gone to get her a glass of lemonade, she heard a familiar voice behind her.

"So you are free at last," Sir Julian said. "I thought that last set was never going to end. I had thought of tripping that boorish fellow you were with and trampling him underfoot so I could take his place."

"I'm glad that you finally made it," Mavis said,

unaware that she had admitted to watching for him. Her partner returned with her drink, but he relinquished the next dance to Sir Julian.

"You look very beautiful," he told her, thinking that she did indeed look a little better. "I thought the rose garden was the perfect setting for you, but you look just as perfect here tonight."

The next dance was a waltz, which Mavis knew she did not do well. She tried to warn Julian before he led her on the floor, but he would accept no excuses. He was determined that she was going to dance with him. Because she was nervous, she tripped several times.

"I'm afraid I'm terribly out of practice," she said apologetically.

"Well, if I hold you tighter, I can guide you much better," he said, and tightened his hold.

Mavis stammered an objection, which was ignored, but she didn't really mind. It was not an unpleasant sensation, having a handsome gentleman holding her close.

"Oh, I did that very badly," Mavis said when the dance finally ended. "I had better find you a good dancing partner, or you'll want to leave immediately."

"If you find me someone else, I'll be sure that you find me totally objectionable, and then I will leave immediately. . . . Do you?" he asked.

"Oh, no," she said. "But I don't dance very well."

"Then let's find something to eat, before we

dance again. That should give you time to regain your courage."

She smiled at him for understanding, then she took his arm and they went to find the tables of food.

Mavis greeted a few people as they went along the corridor, but no one stopped long enough to meet Julian. Just as well, he thought, you could never tell who might have heard of him.

Mavis was rather unsure of herself. She had not been alone like this with a man for several years. She alternated between bursts of quick chatter and nervous silences. Sir Julian squeezed her hand during one of the silences. She really was a nice person, he thought. He had expected someone cold and cynical, but he found instead a touchingly vulnerable woman who seemed much younger than her years. He couldn't imagine where her family had been hiding her for the past years. With the money she was supposed to have, she could have wed long ago. He wondered if her family was really so anxious to marry her off. Robin and Trilby had said they were, but he had seen no sign of it. Maybe it was because those intended suitors had not yet arrived.

There were many different kinds of food to choose from. Sir Julian carried the plates along the buffet and suggested different dishes as they went along. Mavis tried very hard to be agreeable, so her plate was very full by the time they took a table near the wall.

"Is that my plate?" she asked as he put a plate down before her. "Oh, I never meant to have that much! I can't eat all this. What can I do?"

She looked at him, and Julian was surprised by the compassion he felt for her. She really is nervous being here with me, he thought.

"All that dancing has given me a huge appetite," he said with a twinkle in his eye. "If you don't mind, we could switch plates."

"Oh, thank you," she said, quite relieved.

Julian did not actually want much to eat, but he managed to put up a good front. Mavis kept watching him to make sure he was really eating and not just being polite, so he had to finish everything.

"That was good," he said, wiping his mouth after the last lobster patty. He signaled to a waiter for more champagne.

As the waiter left, some women came and sat down at the table next to theirs. Although they were seated very close by, it was impossible to see them because there was a drapery between the tables to give privacy.

"Did you see her?" one of the women asked loudly.

"Yes, I did," another answered. "It was disgraceful. Mavis Tolbert must be thirty, if she's a day, and there she was, prancing around like a young girl."

"Did you notice her dress?" someone asked. "Shocking. So unsuitable."

Julian looked at Mavis's white face. He was really starting to have a good time, and she was just beginning to relax with me, he thought, and those vicious old women had to spoil it. He wished that he could make them suffer for their thoughtlessness, rather than Mavis.

"Could we go, please?" Mavis asked quietly.

He pulled out her chair and she stood up.

"And that man with her, does she really think that he could be interested in her?! Nobody's looked at her for years. Why on earth would someone start now?" the voices continued.

A remark was made that Mavis and Julian could not hear, but from the snickering that followed it, they guessed that it had not been very polite.

Julian moved her away from the table, but instead of going back in the ballroom, he led her outside, into the gardens. They were not very large, but were cool and dark. He guessed from his last look at her face that she would like some time before she had to face others.

They walked along in silence for a few minutes. He could tell by the small sniffs from his side that Mavis had been very hurt by the malicious talk that they had heard. He himself was very angry, much more so than he would have expected. It was not as if she was a sophisticated woman of thirty who would be used to some malicious remarks, he thought. He could tell from the difference in her appearance tonight that she was more attractive than he had at first thought, and the little confidence that she might have gained was no doubt lost now. Well, I'll make sure that she gets it back, he promised himself. I'm not going to let that conversation make any difference to her. He never stopped to wonder why he felt so strongly about it.

They came to a small clearing along the path, and for the moment, they were alone.

"I think you look beautiful tonight," he told her.

"Thank you," she said tearfully.

"If you cry," he said, "you'll get my coat wet, and I could get a terrible chill wearing a damp coat."

"How would I get you wet?" She was so confused by his reasoning that she stopped sniffing.

"Because I'm going to kiss you," he said, moving closer to her. "To do that I'll need to take you in my arms. If you're still crying when I do that, you'll get my coat all soggy."

"Oh, my," was all Mavis could think to say. It was a long time since someone had kissed her. What if she had forgotten how? Would he laugh at her? But then she was in his arms, and she discovered that she hadn't forgotten after all.

Mavis pulled away after a few minutes. Why did he want to kiss her? Was he just being kind because of others' unkindness? That didn't seem like a very good reason, but it was the best that she could come up with. So what? she said to herself as she was pulled once more into his embrace. If he wanted to kiss a plain, thirty-year-old spinster with a "shocking, unsuitable" dress, she wasn't about to ask him for reasons. It was much too pleasant a place to be to wonder why he wanted her there.

* * *

When Kitty heard that Lord Scotney was due to arrive the next day, she made up her mind that she was really going to enjoy herself at the dance. She feared that it might be her last real night of freedom.

Kitty and Alicia had no trouble finding partners, as there was always a shortage of young women at these affairs. The only trouble was, Kitty noticed, she seemed to often find herself dancing with the young boys around Willy's age whose parents brought them to the assemblies to give them practice in correct social behavior.

"You're much nicer than your sister," one such lad confided in her as they waited for the next dance to begin. "She's too tall, makes me feel like a little kid." The young man was only slightly taller than Kitty. "And she frowns all the time. If I made a mistake while I was dancing with her, I think she'd probably tell the whole dance floor about it. . . . You don't even seem to notice. You're a good sport." He led her out onto the floor as the music started.

Wonderful, thought Kitty, all the sixteen-year-old boys around here think I'm a loyal chum, while all their handsome older brothers flock around Alicia. I wager she doesn't frown at them. Kitty was trying out several different scowls that she thought ought to discourage persistent schoolboys, when she noticed her partner looking strangely at her.

"Anything wrong?" he asked. "You're not going

to be sick or anything, are you?" He looked and sounded quite concerned.

"No, I'm fine," said Kitty. She hadn't realized that her thoughts had been reflected on her face.

"That's good," he said. "Father said I have to dance at least four dances tonight, and you're my fourth. So when we're done, I can go find Charlie Langtree and get something to eat. . . . I'm starving," he confided.

The dance was almost over when he stepped on Kitty's skirt, ripping a ruffle near the bottom.

"Gosh, I'm sorry," he said. "I didn't mean to do that." He looked around. "Do you think my mother saw that?" he whispered to Kitty. "She'll skin me if she finds out."

Because his mother was far across the room and didn't look as though she could see two feet in front of her, Kitty assured her young partner that he was probably safe.

"But I'll have to go and fix this," she said. "If I don't, I'll trip on it."

"Couldn't you just finish the rest of the dance first?" he pleaded. "Otherwise, I'll have to dance another whole set."

He looked so pitiful that Kitty felt sorry for him. "The dance is almost over," she told him. "Your parents can't object if your partner was too warm to finish it. . . . Why don't you take me over there, near the lemonade, and get me a glass? Then I can slip out that door and get my skirt fixed."

He looked so relieved that she almost laughed. Was dancing such a terrible trial to him? He led her over to the doorway and procured a large glass of lemonade for her.

"You're a real Trojan," he beamed at her. "I don't even mind dancing with you."

Kitty didn't know how to respond to such high praise, so she just smiled at him and slipped into the hallway, making her way to the room set aside for the ladies' use. A maid would be there to help her with her skirt.

When she found the room, there was another woman there ahead of her, so Kitty sat down by the window to wait her turn. She was in no hurry to return to the ballroom, because her last big night of freedom was not turning out as planned. She hadn't really expected that she would be besieged by hordes of handsome men, all clamoring over her hand for each set, but she would have liked at least one partner who was older than she was. Being a good practice partner for young men learning how to dance was not very romantic.

Kitty saw a couple in the garden below, and her thoughts went off in a different direction. She wondered what it would be like to go out there with a young man. Not the one she had just left, of course. She couldn't imagine him taking a girl out to the garden unless he needed her help in hiding from his parents. But with somebody handsome and a few years older than she was, it might be rather enjoyable.

Kitty wondered what Robin was doing now. She had done fairly well at keeping him out of her mind, but watching the couples in such a romantic setting, her thoughts kept returning to him. It had been quite disappointing to discover that he was no different from any of the "fashionable" people Alicia liked to talk about. She had hoped that he might be here tonight, although she didn't even know if he was still in the area. It was four days since she had last seen him. He could be far away by this time.

Kitty came back to the ballroom very reluctantly. She hoped to avoid her next partner, if she could, and watch the dancers for a while.

"Are you hiding from me?" someone asked her.

Kitty turned around, a wild hope leaping inside her. Robin stood there smiling at her.

"This is my dance, isn't it?" he asked. He started to lead her out to the floor when they heard someone behind him.

"Wait . . . I say there . . . wait!"

They turned to see a very tall, very thin, red-faced young man approaching.

"I say, this is my dance, you know." He tugged at his neckcloth, which was limp and crushed by this time. "Sorry," he said to Robin.

"No, you must be wrong," Robin said to him with a smile that should have daunted him. "This is most definitely my dance." He started to move away with Kitty.

"Please wait," the young man said. "You've got to dance this one with me," he begged Kitty.

"Is this your fourth dance?" she asked him sympathetically.

"No, I've got to do five," he admitted in a funereal voice.

Kitty looked around her. Robin was clearly puzzled by this exchange, but she had promised the dance to this boy and she couldn't just leave him there. She spotted Alicia with a few of her friends, seated near a wall.

"How about Alicia?" she asked.

"She'd never dance with me," he protested.

But Kitty went over to where her sister was sitting.

"Alicia," she asked, "are you free for this dance? There's someone over there who'd like to dance with you." She nodded over to the doorway.

Alicia, whose selective eyesight did not notice tall, thin young men with red faces and rumpled cravats, assumed that Robin was her intended partner.

"Of course, I'm free," she told Kitty and followed her over to where the two men were standing.

The younger man came forward immediately. "Gosh, Miss Alicia," he stammered, "I never thought you'd dance with me."

Before she could recover from her shock and regain the use of her voice, Robin pulled Kitty onto the dance floor and they began to waltz.

"She doesn't look very pleased," Robin reported over Kitty's shoulder.

"Did she leave him there?" Kitty asked.

"No, they're going to dance, but I think he's going to be tempted to do a lot of tugging at his cravat before the dance is done." He looked down at Kitty. "Won't she be angry with you?"

"Yes. Furious probably. But one dance won't hurt her, and I'll take care to stay out of her way until she cools down."

They danced in silence for a few minutes, Robin trying to keep them somewhat in the shadows so he wouldn't be seen much. He had wanted to come to this dance, hoping he would see Kitty again, but he had to be careful not to let the Tolberts know he was there. As much as he would like to be released from the contract, he did not want to involve Kitty.

"I was hoping you would be here tonight," he told Kitty.

"Oh, were you?" Kitty replied. She liked this man and was glad to see him again, but she had to keep reminding herself that he had admitted he was engaged to be married and was in love with someone else, she thought a married woman. Robin might be fun to be with, and it was certainly agreeable to be complimented and sought out, but she must not let herself get too involved with him.

A few minutes later, when the dance was over, Robin spied Alicia bearing down on them. He had no desire to dance with her, as she seemed like the sort who would ask far too many questions. He looked around for a way to escape her.

"Let's get some lemonade," he suggested.

Because every partner she had had so far this evening thought that lemonade was the proper finish to a dance, Kitty was fairly saturated with it, but she had no choice. Robin had a firm hold on her elbow and was directing her steps toward the crowded table in the corner. He got two glasses with ease . . . too much ease, Kitty thought. He must have had a lot of practice at this sort of thing. She wished she had more experience with sophisticated flirting that would leave her heart unhurt.

Robin then led her onto the terrace, where the only lights were some lanterns hung in the trees. He must have felt her hesitation as he led her through the door.

"It's much cooler out here, don't you think?" he asked.

"Oh, yes, it's much better," she said, wondering how he would act toward his fiancée when they were together on a dark terrace.

"Do you have these assemblies often?" he asked after a few minutes' silence.

"In the summer we do," she answered and went back to her lemonade.

Robin watched her in the faint light. He had thought that she was glad to see him when he had arrived, but since then she seemed to be drawing away from him.

Another dance was starting and the other couples on the terrace were drifting back indoors.

"Let's go over here," Robin said, moving her over to a bench hidden by some bushes.

"I've thought a lot about you since the last time we saw each other," he began. Maybe she was still upset by what he had been saying then. Now should be the ideal time to clear it up.

"I was hoping we'd have the chance to be alone like this." He pulled her down by his side on the bench.

She was just watching him, her eyes like deep, dark pools in her face.

"Kitty," he whispered, pulling her close. His lips found hers, and what was meant to be just a gentle kiss grew as he felt her response. Suddenly he felt something cold and wet, running down his chest. He jumped up.

"What the—?" he yelled.

The front of his shirt was all wet. He looked at Kitty.

"My lemonade," she told him in a small voice.

"Your what?" Somehow his whisper seemed like a shout.

She stood up. "It was my glass of lemonade," Kitty tried to explain. "I had it in my hand."

"What was it doing there?" he asked, completely bewildered.

"Where else was it supposed to be?" Kitty was quickly losing her apologetic frame of mind.

"I just wondered why you didn't put it down before I kissed you," he said, quite angry.

"How was I supposed to know that you were going to kiss me?" she demanded. "Oh, I suppose I should have known. What other kind of behavior should I expect from someone who is betrothed to one woman, professes to love another, and takes a third one out into a dark garden to make love to?"

She put her now-empty glass on the bench. "Thank you for the dance, sir," she said, politely curtseying. Her attempt at icy courtesy was spoiled by the rather obvious stomp of her feet as she went back inside.

Why is it nothing works out the way I plan with that girl? Robin asked himself. Here he was, dripping with lemonade, while she went off somewhere, angry at him. How could he go back inside and straighten things out? He could, of course, wait outside here in the hope that she might relent and come back out, but it was too cool a night to stand around in wet clothes. He had just about decided to follow Kitty in and try to wait in some out-of-way place in the hope of talking to her again, when another couple came out.

In the light from the doorway, he recognized Miss Tolbert with a gentleman. Oh, no, he groaned, shrinking into the bushes. There was no way he could go inside now. Suppose Miss Tolbert saw him, disheveled as he was, arguing with Kitty. He didn't mind for himself, but she could make it very difficult for Kitty and hurt her reputation.

Robin went down a secluded path to the stables, where he could get his horse and leave.

Alicia had not regained any measure of charitable feelings for Kitty by the time they were going home.

"Who was that man you were dancing with?" she asked.

Kitty was feeling miserable after leaving Robin and didn't want to explain anything to her sister.

"Why were you hiding him, so I couldn't dance with him?" Alicia persisted.

"Oh, button your lip!" William told her curtly. "Why should all the handsome men at a dance have to stand up with you and not Kitty? She's just as pretty as you are and just as entitled to a good time. So I don't see any need for all this questioning."

William rarely interfered in family squabbles. His doing so now took everyone by surprise. The result was that not only did Alicia keep quiet, but so did everyone in the carriage.

William was not really concerned with whether Alicia or Kitty had a good time, but with someone who quite obviously did. What did Mavis think she was doing? She spent the whole evening, well, almost the whole evening, with that Julian Merriot. The next thing you know, William thought, she'll decide that she's going to get married. Why anyone would want to marry her, he couldn't see, but it would certainly ruin all his plans if she did that now. He was relying on her to get a lot of the details for Kitty's wedding settled. Then he had been hoping to do some hunting up north this autumn, and Mavis had to stay at Crofton Grange with the younger children. He had already made some general inquiries about this Merriot fellow, and it was

148

time to do some real digging. He was not about to let Mavis be tricked into something that was not in her best interest. She'd be much better off at Crofton Grange with the people who really care about her, William told himself, quite pleased with his brotherly concern.

CHAPTER NINE

Kitty had spent all day Monday fretting. She had planned various elaborate and dramatic methods to release herself from the marriage, but she doubted that any of them would work.

Mavis finally suggested that Kitty lie down during the afternoon.

Much to her surprise, Kitty did sleep for a few hours and woke up only when Mavis told her she had to start getting ready. Maggie came in to help her dress.

"This is a big day," Maggie said happily, as she brushed Kitty's hair.

"Yes, it is," agreed Kitty. The beginning of my enslavement, she thought.

By the time that she was fully dressed, Kitty was in a complete state of panic. Maggie left her to help

Alicia and Nellie dress, while Kitty fidgeted at the window. The sound of horses pulling up to the front door made her jump.

Oh, no, she thought, he's here. She walked up and down the length of her room trying to calm her nerves, but it didn't help much. She could hear voices in the front hall.

A drink of water, she told herself, that's what I need. She poured a glass of water from the pitcher on her washstand and tried to drink it. Her throat seemed just as dry afterwards.

She then heard laughter and the sound of people moving into the drawing room. Pacing around and wringing her hands did not help her agitation, and when she heard her father's voice coming up the stairs, her nerves got the best of her.

She ran to the door of her room and looked out. No one was in sight yet. She ran across the hall to the stairs that the servants used and went down quickly. Kitty did not think out what she was doing, but at the last moment, she knew that she could not stay there and meet the horrible person who was marrying her for her money. Her only thought was to get away from the house before her father found her. She followed the terrace that went along the back, so she could not be seen by anyone from an upstairs window. Once around the corner, she would slip down into the garden and quickly be hidden by the tall bushes.

However, when she went around the corner she ran right into someone standing on the terrace. She stepped back, considerably startled, only to become even more unsettled when the person turned around and she saw Robin standing in front of her.

"Kitty," Robin whispered in surprise, "what are you doing here?" He looked over his shoulder.

"Never mind that," he said still in a whisper. He caught hold of her arm and pulled her farther away from the open door he was near. "I've got to talk to you. Why did you run off like that yesterday?" He looked down at her, expecting some sort of response. He was not getting the one he had expected. In fact, he wasn't getting any response at all. She was just staring at him.

"What's the matter with you?" he finally asked her. "For goodness sakes, will you say something?" He kept looking anxiously over his shoulder.

"What are you doing here?" Kitty was surprised that her voice actually did work. She had thought maybe she had taken leave of all her senses and was only imagining him there. An awful thought was taking shape in her mind. She backed away from him and asked again, a little louder this time, "What are you doing here?"

What's the matter with her now? Robin thought. However, he was not given time to answer her question, for at that moment William appeared on the scene.

"Oh, there you are, honey," he said, putting his arm around Kitty. He feared that she was either going to run away or faint. Because Kitty's knees were knocking together at an alarming rate, she wouldn't have been able to move much; but fainting did seem like an acceptable alternative to remaining conscious during the revelation she was almost sure was about to come.

"Well, this is my little girl," William was saying, giving Kitty a hug. "Mary Kathleen. But we just call her Kitty."

"This is Lord Scotney, Kitty," he told her.

What Kitty had already figured out now became clear to Robin. They stared at each other while Robin tried frantically to recall what he had said to Kitty about his intended wife, but he couldn't remember.

Oh, no, Kitty was thinking, was Robin—someone she liked and trusted—actually the hideous Lord Scotney? Was she supposed to be the woman who cared nothing about him, "as long as he didn't die before the wedding"? Would she be expected not to notice while he had his affair with the woman he loved, which her money would probably finance?

At this time, Mavis came out on the terrace. She saw two very pale people staring at each other, while William hugged Kitty.

"I am very happy to meet you," Robin finally murmured to Kitty.

William nudged her, and she curtsied.

"Oh, Mavis," said William, just noticing her, "she was out here all the time." Mavis came forward. "This is my sister, Miss Tolbert."

Robin turned to acknowledge the introduction and saw the woman he had thought he was supposed to marry. She did not look so formidable now. Mavis looked Robin over. He didn't look bad at all, she decided. He might be just the thing for Kitty. He was young, presentable, and looked as ill at ease as Kitty did during this meeting. She decided to give them some help.

"Why don't we go back indoors? It will be cooler out of the sun." Mavis led the way back into the drawing room.

William brought Kitty in and, rather dictatorially, sat her down on the sofa that Robin was heading for. He thought she was shaking so much that she wouldn't be able to change places.

"This has been a hot summer, hasn't it?" Mavis said brightly. Kitty was staring at her hands and said nothing. The Earl murmured his agreement.

"We could use some rain, though," Mavis continued. Kitty was still very pale, and her aunt was determined to chatter as inconsequentially as possible until she had recovered herself slightly.

"Have you had much rain near Scotney Park?" Mavis asked Robin.

He was trying unobtrusively to catch Kitty's eye, but had to turn his attention to Mavis. "Not enough," he said, trying to be polite. He supposed he ought to be conversing more, but he couldn't think of a thing to say to them.

"Have they had much rain in London?" Mavis asked him.

William glared at her. What in the world was she doing? His idea had been to introduce them and then leave them alone for a while to get to know one another. "Who cares about the rain in London?" he grumbled at her.

"Why, I imagine the Londoners care," she said sweetly, as she settled herself back in her chair.

During this interplay, Kitty glanced up at Robin, who had been waiting for such a moment, and he smiled as reassuringly as he could at her. She looked back down quickly, but he thought he had seen the glimmer of a smile first.

"Why don't you two take a walk in the garden?" William suggested to Kitty and Robin.

"Good idea," said Robin as he jumped up. Here was a chance to talk to Kitty and tell her how delighted he was that she had turned out to be the Miss Tolbert of the contract.

"Oh, no," said Kitty, equally firm. "It's too hot out there. I don't really feel like walking in the hot sun." What she didn't feel like was being alone with Robin. Not yet. She was still too confused by her feelings.

"She's right, William," Mavis insisted, as William's mouth opened to override his daughter. "Just look how pale she is. She wouldn't last more than a few minutes out there."

Robin sat down again. It was true that Kitty was very pale. He couldn't very well insist that they go outside if she was on the verge of fainting.

William went back to glaring at Mavis. What had gotten into her lately? She had changed, and he feared it was not for the better.

"Why don't you pour us some sherry?" Mavis suggested.

He got up and went over to the decanter on a side table.

He poured the glasses and passed them around. Then Alicia, Nellie, and Willy came into the room. William introduced them to Lord Scotney. Willy was not impressed and sat down near Nellie and tried to talk to her. Nellie was watching Kitty, though, hoping to get a clue to her feelings. Alicia chose a chair near Robin to talk with him. She asked him about several people who had figured prominently in the social columns of the London newspapers, but he knew few of them. He was not even very knowing of the latest scandals. If he wasn't an Earl, Alicia sighed to herself, he wouldn't be worth the trouble.

"Where's Tim?" William asked.

"He left for school with Mr. Bowen, this morning," Nellie reminded him.

"Oh, that's right." He gave an embarrassed laugh. "Sometimes it's hard to keep track of them all."

William took Mavis into dinner, while Kitty went in with Robin. He took advantage of their slight separation from the others to whisper to her.

"Why didn't you tell me your real name?" he asked.

"You didn't tell me the truth about yourself, either," she replied curtly. Why did the first thing he said to her after learning the truth have to remind her of her past escapades?

It was hard for Kitty to throw away all of her objections to the marriage just because Robin turned out to be fairly polite and handsome. She kept remembering the things he had said about his intended wife and about the woman he loved. But then, he did seek her out at the assembly, before he knew her identity, so maybe he did like her for herself.

They were seated rather informally around the table. William was at the head, and Mavis at the foot, with Robin on William's right and Kitty next to him. Across the table sat Alicia, Willy, and Nellie. Although it was considered impolite to talk across the table, Alicia did, because she was convinced that an Earl should be tremendously interesting. Just because he was not up on the latest stories from London did not make him a nodcock.

Kitty spoke to Robin only a few times at the table, and then only when he addressed a remark to her. Because they were not supposed to have met previously, he could not refer to any earlier meeting or make any even slightly personal remark. It severely restricted conversation.

It was not noticed, however, that Kitty was rather silent, because her father talked incessantly. The fact that he had a real Earl eating at his table had awakened a loquacious vein in his body that he hadn't known existed. He talked about everything from hunting to the war with France and the current styles of fashion. (Alicia could have told him to skip that last subject, because Lord Scotney was certainly not dressed as a leader of fashion.) William went on, regardless of the response, or lack of it.

In an attempt not to show how impressed he really was by Robin's title, William was trying to be very chummy. He felt that, as a sophisticated man-of-the-world, he should treat Robin as he would any young man who came to see one of his daughters. The fact that his behavior this evening was totally unlike his normal behavior had escaped him. He thought he was being his normal, friendly self.

All the talking was tiring, however, and he began to run down slightly as the dessert was served. Once the women had left, William was able to revive his lagging spirits with four glasses of port, and when the men rejoined the ladies, he was ready to be charming once more.

"How about some music, girls?" he suggested.

Alicia got up and started for the pianoforte, but William stopped her.

"No, no," he said. "It's Kitty's big night. Let her go first."

Kitty would have rather turned somersaults across the room while singing lewd drinking songs than play for an audience, and she considered anyone besides herself an audience. She got up slowly and went to choose some music.

"Play something romantic," William said, with a grin at Robin.

Robin, remembering what Kitty had once said about her musical skills, hoped that it would be something short, for her sake. Personally, he was so delighted with the way things had turned out that he didn't mind having to listen to her, no matter how badly she played.

Kitty began to play the two songs that she had

chosen. The words seemed faintly familiar, but the music was unrecognizable. When she was finished, she returned quickly to her place, and Alicia went up to play.

"Are you going to sing with me, Kitty?" Alicia asked. Kitty shook her head, as Nellie went up to join Alicia.

Under the cover of Alicia's playing, Robin leaned toward Kitty.

"I enjoyed hearing you play," he said quietly.

"Thank you," she replied, pretending to be listening closely to her sister's performance. Oh, how could he lie like that? Kitty thought. Her playing was awful. Either he thought she was really naive, and would believe anything, or else he was laughing at her inexpertness and thought it a good joke. Neither possibility was very comforting.

Alicia was playing her best tonight. She felt that she finally had an audience worthy of her. It was unfortunate that it was so good, however, because it made Kitty's seem even worse.

"It's such a relief to hear you play, after Kitty's pounding," William said when Alicia had finished her first song. "I forgot how terribly Kitty plays or I wouldn't have subjected our guest to it." He turned toward Robin. "My apologies, sir. I promise to keep her away from the keyboard any time you're here." He chuckled at his own joke.

Robin was amazed at William's lack of sensitivity. Kitty had obviously not wanted to play, and she knew how bad it had sounded. Now he was humiliating her further by calling everyone's attention to how well Alicia played.

"I didn't think it was so bad," Robin said, trying to make Kitty feel better. But she glared at him as if he had insulted her more than her father had.

"It's too bad," William continued. "Alicia has all the talent, but Kitty has the fortune." He chuckled some more. "But you can't complain," he told Robin confidentially. "Once you get your hands on her money, you can hire people to do all the things that she can't." He roared at his own wit, while the others stared at him.

Robin felt an almost uncontrollable desire to plant him a facer and wondered if it was a proper thing to do to one's future father-in-law. He was also beginning to understand Kitty's lack of enthusiasm for marrying him. If he had always been discussed as someone who only wanted her money, it was not surprising that she wouldn't even look at him. He had conveniently forgotten his own hesitations.

Nellie and Alicia suddenly began to talk very loudly to cover up their embarrassment. Even Alicia had been horrified by her father's rudeness, not because Kitty had been embarrassed, but because it was not proper for her father to mention Kitty's money like that.

Nellie suggested a game of lottery tickets, and Robin agreed. Alicia joined in so that the Earl would not think that they were lacking in good manners. Kitty just followed the others silently.

Lottery tickets was definitely not Robin's favorite game, but he felt they all needed something to do. If they were unoccupied, William might continue to display his complete lack of brains.

Robin liked Nellie and Willy. They were both easygoing and unpretentious. Neither one was impressed with his title, which was fine with him. Alicia was different, though. She was everything the others were not. He had met a large number of young women like her in London. Each tried to be more fashionable and more sophisticated than the next one. Yet they were all equally boring and tiresome.

Robin decided to leave soon afterwards.

"Thank you for the dinner," he told William. He said good night to Kitty and the others. When he thanked them for a pleasant evening, Kitty felt like crying, but she answered him quite properly.

"Why don't you come and take her riding tomorrow?" William suggested. "We can seat you, if you don't have your own mount along."

"I'd like to," Robin replied, looking at Kitty. She gave him no clue as to her feelings in the matter, and because it was dark in the hallway, he couldn't judge by her expression.

"Good night," he said again, and then went out.

Kitty's hopes of a peaceful night, when she would have time to think things out, were spoiled as Alicia came into her room just as Kitty was climbing into bed.

"You're a sly one," Alicia said. "I never dreamed

that your mysterious friend at the assembly was actually your Earl! Meeting him in secret like that! And I was afraid you would never make it in London society . . . But why didn't you tell me? I'd have understood." She settled herself at the foot of Kitty's bed.

"But I wasn't meeting him in secret," Kitty protested. "I didn't know who he was."

"Oh, you'll do fine in London, with your escorts and flirts, but you must find out who they are, Kitty," Alicia laughed. "Think how awful it would be if your clandestine lover turned out to be your husband!" She laughed even harder. "I would not have expected you to be sneaking out to see a man; I had thought you were too provincial. But it's good to see that you'll be able to adapt well to your married life."

Kitty could not believe what Alicia was saying! Did Alicia really think that she was having clandestine meetings with different men? "But we only met accidentally, Alicia," Kitty insisted. "He didn't know who I was and I didn't know him. He was surprised tonight to find out who I really was. I wasn't sneaking around with any men."

Alicia laughed even harder. "Maybe you really are the provincial I thought you were, but Lord Scotney certainly isn't. Do you really believe that your meeting was accidental? Oh, come on, Kitty! Use your head! A man of the world like Lord Scotney isn't going to come down here and marry somebody he's never seen, no matter how much money she has. He's going to at least come down first and see what she's like." When Kitty didn't say anything, Alicia continued. "You may not have known who he was, but he certainly knew who you were. Why else would he seek you out at the assembly last night? He wanted to see what you were like. Goodness! An Earl would have to marry someone presentable. Suppose you were a fat, ugly thing, with no sense of fashion or proper behavior. You have to do him credit, you know. You'll be his hostess and entertain his friends. He would want to make sure that you were young enough to give him an heir. He wouldn't want his title to die out because you were too old to bear children. Depend on it, Kitty. He knew who you were."

Kitty shifted her position on the bed. "But he's very handsome," Alicia went on. "With your money, he'll be able to keep himself in style and wear more fashionable clothes . . . Oh, it'll be a fabulous life," Alicia sighed. "How I envy you!" She shrugged her shoulders at Kitty's lack of response. "Well, I must be off to bed." She stood up. "Sleep well, Kitty."

After Alicia left, Kitty thought for a few minutes about what her sister had said. Could it be true that Robin had known all along who she was? The things that Alicia said made sense—too much sense. It was all so depressing! Why couldn't she just fall in love and marry someone of her own choice? Why did she have to fall in love with a cad . . . a bounder . . . a fortune hunter whom her father had bought for her? That was the whole problem, she admitted to herself. She was in love with

Robin, and she had thought that he liked her. But what did she know about men? Was it all a game to him? Could she trust him? What about the woman he said he loved?

Kitty was about to extinguish the candle by her bed when she heard a knock at her door. Nellie stuck her head in.

"Good, you're not asleep yet." She came in all the way and closed the door.

"Oh, Kitty, isn't he handsome!" she exclaimed as she climbed up on the bed. "You're so lucky. He's really nice." She noticed Kitty's downcast expression but misinterpreted the reason for it. "Oh, don't be upset by what Father said. It was horrible, but Lord Scotney didn't like it either. He looked like he was very angry with Father. . . . What's wrong, Kitty?" Nellie sank back against the bedpost. "Didn't you like him?"

"Yes, he seems nice," Kitty admitted. "But I don't think I'm going to marry him. I don't know what I should do." She seemed so near tears that Nellie was alarmed. She had envisioned a happy little coze tonight, not a sad, depressing session.

"What's the matter, Kitty?" she asked.

Kitty was upset by what Alicia had said and could no longer think clearly, so she decided to confide in Nellie.

"Well, you see," she began, "I met him before, accidentally, at the assembly." She didn't want to explain all those other meetings. "And he was very nice, and I thought he didn't know who I was because I didn't know who he was, except that

163

Alicia says he must have because he's not a provincial like me." Kitty stopped for a breath.

"What?" Nellie asked feebly. "Where does Alicia come into this?"

"Well, she saw him at the assembly and wanted to dance with him, except that he wanted to dance with me instead."

"That's not surprising. I would think most men would rather dance with you than with her."

Kitty smiled at her. "Thanks," she said. "But, you see, Alicia says he only sought me out because he knew who I was, even though I didn't know him."

"How could you dance with him if you didn't know him?" Nellie asked.

"That's not the point," Kitty said impatiently. "I knew his name, but not his title." She settled back on the pillows. "Oh, Nellie, I'm so confused. I thought that he was nice, but he's in love with somebody else; and now Alicia says he knew who I was all along."

"How do you know he's in love with someone else? It doesn't seem like the sort of thing he would tell you." Nellie was having trouble making sense of what Kitty was saying.

Kitty didn't want to admit that he had in fact told her—it would involve too many explanations of when he told her—so she said, "I heard him tell someone." Nellie gave her a strange look. "Does it really matter how I know? The thing is, I know he's in love with someone else, and he's supposed to marry me. . . . Do you think Alicia's right and that he knew it was me all along? She made it sound like he came down to check out the merchandise before he bought it," she said bitterly.

"Maybe he did want to see what you were like; that's not so horrible, is it?" Nellie asked.

"But why not come to the house openly? Why was it all so secretive? Unless he didn't want Father to know he was here yet."

"That could be it," Nellie said excitedly. "Maybe he hoped to talk to you privately. If he's in love with someone else, he might have hoped to persuade you to call off the wedding."

"But he didn't ask me," Kitty said. "He never admitted knowing who I was."

"Well." Nellie was thinking hard. "Maybe once he met you, he didn't want to ask you. Maybe he thought you were innocent and vulnerable and needed someone to protect you." Nellie was enjoying herself, embellishing her story as she went along. "Maybe he found he just couldn't tell you, and then he decided he had to go through with the wedding. Even now the woman he loves may be waiting to hear from him, hoping that he was released from his contract so they could marry." Nellie searched for a handkerchief in the pocket of her robe and blew her nose.

Oh, it could be true, Kitty thought. After the cockfight, he was awfully angry. Suppose he thought then that I was too innocent and needed a husband to look after me. Or, worse still, maybe he felt he had compromised me by taking me to that fight and had no choice but to marry me.

Maybe, at this very moment, he was with her. Well, not actually with her, whispering to her through her window, telling her he would have to marry me. Kitty remembered the humiliations of the evening. "After everything that happened tonight, he probably feels so sorry for me that he'll never tell me the truth," Kitty said.

"He's being so brave," Nellie cried. "Sacrificing his own love . . ." She had to stop because she was crying so hard.

"I can't let him do it," Kitty sobbed. "He's too nice a person. I'll have to sacrifice my own feelings. I'll make up some story to tell him, but I'll get him out of the contract. He'll never know how much it hurt me, but at least he'll be free and can be happy."

The idea of Robin being happy while Kitty was miserable made the girls cry even harder. It was their idea of the perfect romance. The only trouble was, Kitty didn't feel very happy about it because she didn't really want to give Robin up to someone else.

"If he loves another," she told Nellie dramatically, "I cannot stand in his way."

Nellie nodded, mopping her eyes with the edge of the sheet, having already soaked her small, lace-trimmed handkerchief.

"I thought I heard voices."

The girls looked up. Aunt Mavis stood in the doorway. "What is going on in here?" she demanded. "Both of you should be in bed, asleep.

Nellie, go to bed . . . right now," she added as Nellie hesitated.

When Nellie left, Mavis looked at Kitty, taking in the new tears. "Get a good night's sleep," she said gently. "We'll talk more tomorrow." She blew out the candle near Kitty's bed and went out, leaving Kitty crying quietly in the dark, sure that she had solved the puzzle of Robin's behavior. All that remained was for her to be brave and follow through with her resolution.

Mavis met Kitty in the hall after breakfast. "You had better change, Kitty," she said. "Lord Scotney will be here soon."

"I was hoping we could walk in the gardens instead," Kitty said. "You know how badly I ride, even though I practice a lot. I don't want him to think I couldn't do anything well."

"I'm not sure that walking in the garden is a tremendously valuable talent to possess," Mavis said. "But I do understand why you don't want to go riding. Why don't you go freshen up? He'll be here soon."

CHAPTER TEN

Robin was no longer despondent about his forth-coming marriage and was eagerly awaiting his chance to talk to Kitty privately. He had decided that the best course for him to take was total honesty. He'd tell her how his father had never mentioned the marriage and how he had delayed coming in hopes that something would happen to prevent it. After he had helped her out of the bushes, he wanted even less to go through with the marriage. Finally, he was delighted with the way things had worked out and he would try very hard to make her happy.

Robin had practiced his speech while he was riding to Crofton Grange, and he was confident that he would convince her of his sincerity. He had decided not to tell her he loved her yet. After all, he told himself, she was not very experienced with men. She would probably like a little time to get used to the idea of marrying him before he complicated it with his feelings.

When Robin arrived, Mavis greeted him and showed him into a sitting room, while she had a footman get Kitty. They made polite conversation for a few minutes, until Kitty came down.

Robin stood up as Kitty entered the room. She was wearing a soft, green muslin that looked very cool in spite of the heat outside. Her dark hair was pinned up very simply and held back with a matching green ribbon.

"Good morning," Robin said.

Kitty smiled nervously. "Hello," she said, thinking it was not going to be as easy as she had thought.

She looked around the room, but Mavis had disappeared, leaving the two of them alone.

"I thought we could walk in the garden, instead of riding," Kitty explained, adding, "I'm not a very good rider."

"I'd like that," Robin assured her, ". . . walking in the garden, I mean."

Kitty opened the French doors at the far end of the room, and they walked onto the terrace.

They were both quiet as they started down the path. Robin thought Kitty seemed more composed this morning, which should have been a good sign, except she didn't seem as relaxed as she had been when they had met before. Well, maybe that was to be expected. After all, who knows what nonsense her father had been telling her all these years about Lord Scotney? However, try as he might, he couldn't remember how he had planned to begin his rehearsed speech. Every time that he looked at Kitty, which was fairly often, he forgot everything else.

"Kitty," he said at last, "I'm glad we finally have this chance to talk alone together." He stopped walking and turned toward her.

Kitty was rapidly losing her composure. She opened her mouth several times to tell him she wasn't going to marry him, but nothing came out.

He moved closer to her and took one of her hands. "Kitty . . ." he began.

All her resolutions rapidly disappeared when he was close to her. She stepped back, trying hard to remember her decision, and found herself ankle-deep in mud.

"Oh, my," she said in dismay. Robin let go of her hand, and she gingerly stepped back on the path. Her shoes were wet and streaked with mud. She held her dress up so that it wouldn't touch her shoes, and stared at them.

Robin looked at her blankly for a few minutes. He didn't think that wet, muddy shoes were conducive to romance. "Maybe you'd better change them," he finally suggested. "I'll just wait out here for you." He indicated the terrace.

Kitty swallowed hard. The time had come for her to speak.

"No, you don't have to wait," she said. She looked down at the path, while her hands tightly clutched the muslin of her dress. She glanced briefly up at his face. He was staring at her in surprise. "I wanted to tell you last night, but I never got the chance. . . . You see, I told my father all along that I wouldn't marry you, but he wouldn't listen to me." She swallowed again and hurried on. "But I did mean it. You've been very polite and gentlemanly, and I do like you, but I will not marry you."

She took a few small steps backward toward the house as her resolution was draining away. "Maybe, if you could tell Father . . . I thought he might listen more to you." She took one last look at Robin's bewildered face and ran up the stairs, across the terrace, and into the house. She heard Robin call her name, but she didn't stop.

In the hallway, Kitty barely missed running into Mavis, who was leaving the library.

"Well," Mavis asked, "was Lord Scotney impressed with your ability to walk in the garden?" She stopped as she took in fully the picture before her. Kitty's hair was falling down, her dress was crumpled in her hands, and two very muddy shoes could be seen beneath the muslin.

"What happened this time?" she asked. Then seeing Kitty's face clearly showing her distress, she said, "Never mind now. Go change your shoes and fix your hair. Come down to the sitting room when you're ready." Mavis gave her an encouraging smile and went off toward the gardens. Through the window, she could see that Lord Scotney had been joined by Willy, so she decided to stay in the house and wait for Kitty.

Kitty's announcement had thoroughly shaken Robin, although, he told himself, he shouldn't have been surprised. He had already guessed that Mr. Tolbert had not been very tactful in his references to the marriage. He was still sure that he could convince her that she should marry him, but he had changed his plan. When she came back down, he would throw caution to the winds and tell her that he loved her. He would admit that he had loved her since that first day when she had fallen into the bushes. She would have to believe him.

Willy came out before Kitty did and offered to show Robin his new stallion, of which he was quite proud. Robin agreed and was led off toward the stables.

"He's a real beauty," Willy said. "Fastest horse we've got here." He looked around him as if he remembered something. "Where's Kitty? I thought you came here to see her."

"She got some mud on her shoes," Robin explained, "and went to change them."

They reached the stables and Willy proudly showed his horse. While Robin examined him and exclaimed about his size and beauty, Willy watched him. He's not a bad fellow, Willy thought. He couldn't see why Kitty objected to him. Nellie had told him, just this morning, though, that Kitty was still determined not to marry him. Willy shrugged his shoulders as they left the stables and started back toward the house. He had promised to help if he could, even if he didn't understand the need for it.

"Was Kitty acting all right this morning?" Willy asked.

"Acting all right?" Robin was confused. What concern were Kitty's manners to her younger brother?

"Well . . . I mean . . . did she seem normal?" Willy tried to explain.

"Normal?" Robin asked blankly.

"Sometimes she gets kind of strange," Willy said. "You know, she acts different, doesn't make too much sense when she talks."

Robin found that much of what Kitty said didn't make sense, but he never would have classified her as strange.

Willy looked embarrassed. "She takes after her grandmother . . . on our mother's side. She was really . . . strange. Kitty was named for her, you know." He looked at Robin, wishing he had never begun this. It had been the only idea he had come up with, but so far Robin didn't look too worried that he might acquire a crazy wife.

"She used to sell boats," Willy continued.

"Kitty?"

"No, no, our grandmother." Willy feared he was really making a mess of this. "She used to get little boats, dinghies, and rename them with fancy names, like Egyptian Queen and the Golden Seahawk. Then she'd sell them to people who thought they were big ships. Made a lot of money that way but got herself into all sorts of trouble too. She was arrested once, but no one had any proof that she had cheated them. Then she decided to sell trees. Big, fully grown ones on her property. People could come and pick out a tree, and she would sell it to them; but they had to leave it growing there. Not too many people bought any. The last thing she decided to do, when she was eighty-one, was become an opera dancer. She traveled to Dublin to find a job as one, but she got sick on the journey down. Eventually died from it, but everybody said she was really crazy . . . and Kitty looks just like her. Father's afraid that she inherited more than just her looks from Granny, and that's why he's so anxious to get her married fast. Wouldn't want you to suspect the truth."

Willy looked to see if Robin was believing much of this, but it was hard to tell. "I didn't think it was fair," Willy went on, "not to tell you the truth. In case Kitty was . . . strange, too." Willy stopped. How had he let Nellie talk him into this?

Robin looked very serious, which required a great deal of effort on his part. "I will be extremely watchful," Robin assured Willy, "especially if Kitty tries to sell me a boat or a tree."

Willy hurried off, still not sure of Lord Scotney's reaction. Robin sat down on the terrace to wait for Kitty. He wondered who had come up with that story. He smiled as he thought of it. Was she really that determined not to marry him? It might take a bit more convincing than he thought. He wished she'd come down; he was impatient to begin his persuasion.

He heard a soft step behind him and jumped up, hoping that Kitty had returned at last. It was Nellie.

"Good morning," he said pleasantly. His confidence was returning.

"Hello," she smiled. She looked at him for a moment and then asked, "Could we walk a little in

174

the garden? I would like to talk to you if I might."

"Certainly," Robin said. "Just point out the way you want to go." He offered his arm, but she refused it with an embarrassed look. He followed her down the steps. Was it her turn to persuade him not to marry Kitty?

"I hope you won't think I'm interfering," Nellie said.

"Please feel free to tell me anything you want," he assured her as they started down a path that was new to him. At least he was seeing a lot of the garden this morning.

Nellie had put a great deal of thought into this plan and was sure that it was foolproof. It had come to her in a moment of inspiration just a little while ago, so she had not been able to tell Kitty of her brilliance yet; but she knew her sister would be impressed by the results she would get.

"It's about Edward," Nellie began.

"Who's Edward?" Robin asked, wondering if this was her grandfather, or maybe a cousin who had done something "strange."

"He's the one Kitty really wants to marry." Nellie paused for effect. Reading all those novels has really paid off, she thought. It gives one the necessary feel for drama.

Robin felt as if the floor had dropped out from under him. The humor with which he had been viewing the interview rapidly vanished.

"Maybe you'd better tell me about him," he said.

Nellie looked at him, quite pleased with the effect of her announcement. "Kitty met him when she was in Brighton with our Aunt Sally. They fell in love immediately, but Father won't even let him come to see her," she said sadly, getting more involved in her story.

"Why not? Is he ineligible?" Robin asked.

"Oh, no, he's quite unexceptional. He has a handsome establishment in Kent and a home in London." She paused again. Robin felt a cold horror growing in him. "It's because of you," Nellie continued. "You see, Father always said that Kitty was to marry you. Edward has no title. . . . He has a comfortable income, but no title."

The horror was rapidly increasing. Things began to fall into place. Nellie continued, apparently oblivious to Robin's distress. "She always told Father she didn't want to marry you. . . . Well, it was your brother before . . . but Father kept insisting. I thought you might understand." She looked up at him with what she thought was a sincere look. "It's breaking her heart."

They reached a small bench and sat down. Nellie was a bit puzzled by his reaction. She had expected him to be surprised and concerned, perhaps, but surely he could see that this was his way out?

"Maybe if you could talk to Father," Nellie hinted, "tell him you don't think you and Kitty are well suited. He'd listen to you." There wasn't much response. "Then you'd both be free," she added. That last remark was a little crude, she feared, but he definitely was not very fast at thinking things through. Couldn't he see, if the contract was broken, he would be free to marry his true love? Nellie began to get excited again at the prospect of helping the course of true love, but she didn't get a chance to add to the story more. Robin had stood up.

"I'll talk to him," Robin promised. "I'll make sure the wedding is cancelled." He started back.

"You mustn't mention Edward to Father," Nellie warned him. "He won't listen then."

"No, I won't mention him," Robin assured her. "I don't think I'll need to." He gave her a rather weak smile. "Thank you for being honest with me. I will do what I can to help Kitty; I promise."

"Thank you for being so understanding," Nellie said, delighted with her success.

Robin did not share her delight. In fact, he could not remember ever being so despondent. He had been so sure that Kitty was objecting to the marriage because it was being forced on her. He had never dreamed that she was actually in love with someone else. He had been convinced that he would eventually win her over, but he saw there was no chance of that now. His presence was just making things harder for her, and he was determined to remove himself. He could do that much for her, if nothing else.

He walked up the steps to the terrace, looking for someone to direct him to William. He thought it would be best to tell him right away.

Robin entered the drawing room and found Kitty sitting there. He had not planned to talk to her again but decided to take the opportunity to re-assure her.

"I didn't realize that you were still here," she said, rising from her chair.

"Please sit," he said, as he took the chair opposite her. "Willy dragged me off to see his prize possession," he said with a smile.

"Oh, yes, his new horse," she replied. "He's quite proud of it."

There were a few moments of silence in which Kitty studied her hands carefully.

Then Robin said, "I want you to know that I'm not going to pressure you into reconsidering your decision. I realize that it would only distress you, and that is not my desire. I accept your wishes, and I'm glad that you were honest with me about them." He gave her a quick smile, because she seemed so quiet. "I'd like to talk to your father this morning, before I leave. Maybe you could tell me where I could find him."

"I think he's in the library," Kitty told him.

He took her hand and slowly raised it to his lips. "Don't worry," he said. "I'll fix everything for you. You won't be bothered with me anymore." He bowed slightly and left the room. Kitty heard him walk across the hall and knock at the door of the library.

She sat still, staring at her hand, where he had kissed her. Tears started running down her cheeks and fell onto her dress, making dark green blotches.

"It was all true, then," she whispered to herself.

"He really does love someone else. . . . He said he was glad that I was honest with him. He was glad to find a way out."

She suddenly realized that she had been talking out loud and looked quickly around her, but no one was in sight. She got up and went to the hall doorway. Robin was in the library, no doubt convincing her father that he shouldn't marry her.

The house was very still as Kitty ran up to her room and locked the door after her. This was one time when she had no desire to talk to Nellie or anyone.

Robin rode off in a particularly foul mood and hoped he would meet no one. The meeting with William had gone very badly. He truly loved Kitty, and the best thing he could do for her was not to marry her; but even in that small thing, he had failed. William was quite adamant. The marriage between them would take place as planned. There would be no excuses. Nothing would stop it. The worst thing was that he had given Kitty his promise that he would settle things with her father. Right now she was probably happily planning her future with the lucky Edward, he thought bitterly, believing that Robin would keep his promise.

Robin had wanted to talk to Kitty after he had talked with her father, but William had forbidden it. Robin deeply regretted that he had not been able to break the news to her. Leaving like this was the coward's way out.

He pulled his horse around. There was a small

chance that Kitty might decide to go out riding today, and he might see her if he waited in the vicinity. Because he could think of no other spot, he returned to the place they had first met, by the creek. He tied his horse near the water, then sat down on the wall to wait.

After lunch, Mavis went to her room to collect a book and then into the gardens to find a cool spot to read. She found a bench in the shade and settled back to enjoy her book.

"Hello, Mavis."

Mavis opened her eyes at the sound of the quiet voice, and for a moment she could not remember where she was.

"Goodness," she said, considerably startled by the sight of Sir Julian standing in front of her. "Oh, my," she said, looking for her book and wondering how he had managed to sneak up on her like that. She frantically felt her hair, which seemed rather disarranged.

"I didn't mean to startle you," Julian said as he captured one of her hands and sat down next to her. "You were sleeping so peacefully that I hated to wake you." He smiled at her. "But I came all the way over here to see you, and I hated to leave without doing so."

"I'm so glad that you came by," Mavis said. "I just didn't plan to fall asleep, you see. I don't usually do that sort of thing." She looked at him for understanding. "I thought that only old ladies fell asleep in gardens.

"Nonsense," laughed Julian. "Why I once fell asleep in a garden, and I didn't have the excuse of being by myself with a book. I was attending a large garden party filled with supposedly witty and amusing people. I was so bored and uncomfortably hot that when I relaxed on a bench in a cool, secluded spot, I immediately fell asleep. Unfortunately, I did not awaken until after all the other guests had left. The servants were cleaning up the yard, and I had hoped to slip out unobserved; but the host and hostess were supervising the operation while discussing the success of the party. I had to go to them and thank them for a delightful time, while they wondered why I was still there, hours after the last guest had left."

Mavis was laughing so hard she could barely speak. "What did they say to you?"

"Well, they were too well bred to come right out and ask me where I had been, so they merely expressed their pleasure that I had come and had enjoyed myself."

"But did you?"

"Enjoy myself? Oh, yes. It was one of the pleasantest afternoons I had had for weeks. A refreshing nap in a cool garden is just the thing for restoring one's spirits. However, I neglected to tell all that to my host. I became haughty and titled, and they did not dare press me for details."

Julian was glad to see that she had forgotten her earlier embarrassment. He watched her as she laughed unaffectedly, remembering the girls whom he had met in London. They were all afraid to laugh. They would smile, or giggle, or even titter embarrassedly, but none of them actually laughed as if she were enjoying herself.

"Oh, my," sighed Mavis as she wiped her eyes. "I think you must have made that up. You don't look like the sort of person who would fall asleep at a party."

"Does that mean that you think I only enjoy myself when I'm going to parties?" asked Julian, not sure that he liked that image.

"Oh, no," said Mavis. "I just meant that you seemed too polite to do that. Surely it is not the proper thing to do."

"I promise you that I have never done it since then," Julian assured her. "I would have come over to see you yesterday," Julian told her. "But Mr. Winfield had invited me out with him, and I couldn't refuse."

"I never expected you to come yesterday," she said. "I am glad to see you, though."

No, thought Julian, she probably didn't think I would come. Someone has done a very effective job of stomping down her self-confidence, so she never expects any attention.

"Could we walk a little?" he suggested.

"Oh certainly," she agreed. Mavis stood up and discovered that her book had slid down under the edge of her skirt. Julian picked it up and offered to carry it for her. Although he was afraid he might be rushing things, he had decided to put his luck to the test. A rather nasty letter he had received this morning was forcing him to abandon the luxury of a slower courtship.

"I enjoyed your company at the assembly Sunday night," he told her.

"I had a good time, too," Mavis said. "I can't remember the last time I enjoyed myself as much."

Julian smiled at her. She was so inexperienced that she forgot to hide her true feelings like most young girls today. It was a very pleasant change.

"It seems to me," Julian continued, "that we get along very comfortably together."

"Yes," Mavis hesitated, suddenly unsure of where the conversation was heading. "I guess that we do."

He stopped walking and turned toward her. "Have you ever thought we might let this relationship continue?"

"No," Mavis answered.

"No?" asked Julian considerably surprised.

"No, I hadn't thought about it," Mavis explained. "It never occured to me that it might continue," she said quietly. He certainly was not suggesting something improper, was he? She had always assumed that men made illicit propositions to ravishingly beautiful women, not to someone as plain as she was. If she had some hidden sexual magnetism, it had remained very well hidden during the last ten years. It suddenly dawned on her that Julian had spoken again.

"What did you say?" she asked him.

"I asked you to marry me, Mavis," Julian told her. This was not his usual proposal. He had never had to repeat himself because the lady was not listening.

"Marry you?" Mavis said in surprise. "Me? . . . You want to marry me?" Why would he want to marry her?

"What did you think I was leading up to?" he asked irritably.

"Well, I didn't know," said Mavis, rather embarrassed. "That's what I was trying to figure out when I wasn't paying attention. . . . It never occurred to me that you were proposing marriage, and I couldn't believe that you would want to propose anything else to me." She was horribly embarrassed by the way the conversation was going and found herself staring at the tips of her shoes, which peeked out from under her dress.

"Well, that's a fine opinion you have of me," Julian said, not at all kindly. "I'm aware that you don't think much of yourself, but I didn't think you would apply the same standard to everyone who tries to be polite to you. All I was trying to do was make an honest proposal of marriage, not try to arrange some sordid relationship. But maybe you are too set in your colorless life to want to take a chance on any kind of association. If that's so I'm sorry I bothered you."

Julian stopped for a minute and looked at her. She still stood with her head bent, apparently studying her shoes. She didn't look up or say anything. Well, that did it, Julian thought. I've ruined everything by getting angry at her. Now she won't even look at me. He told himself the feeling of desolation that he was experiencing was due solely to the fact that he had many bills that were past due, and he had placed all of his hopes on Mavis's fortune. He could apologize, but he wasn't really sorry. He was angry at the way she let everyone walk all over her and expected nothing in return, but why should he care?

"Here's your book," he told her, holding it out. "I had better go." She held out her hand and he placed the book in it, but he hesitated to leave. Wouldn't she say anything to him? "Well, goodbye, then," he said and started to turn away.

"Julian."

It was barely a whisper. If he hadn't been listening for some sign from her, he would have missed it. He turned back to her. She looked up and he saw that she was trying not to cry. The hurt and fear that he saw in her face at the assembly were nothing compared to what he saw there now, and he knew that he had caused it.

"Please . . . Don't go," she tried to say.

He pulled her into his arms, holding her tightly, and for the third time in less than a week, the calm, composed Miss Tolbert burst into tears.

"Don't cry, Mavis," he pleaded. "I'm sorry. I never meant to hurt you." If she was the one who had been hurt, why was it that he was feeling so awful? "I just get so angry when you let everyone take advantage of you and don't think you are worth anything. You are. Do you hear me?" he asked, shaking her a little. "You're worth a great deal to me, and I don't want any more of this nonsense. Do you understand?"

Mavis had not stopped crying, but she had slowed down so she could hear what Julian was saying. She nodded in answer to his question. He held her tightly, in silence, for a few more minutes. When it seemed that most of the tears had passed, he moved away from her slightly. Pulling out his handkerchief, he gently wiped her eyes.

"You never did answer me, you know."

She looked at him questioningly.

"Mavis," he said quietly, but a trifle impatiently, "will you marry me?"

Before she got a chance to answer, he pulled her into his arms again and proceeded to kiss her very thoroughly. When he was finished, he looked down at her.

"That's in case you are still wondering why I'm asking you," he said with an alarming gleam in his eye. He kissed her again, more gently this time. "Say yes, Mavis," he whispered against her lips. "Say you'll marry me."

"Yes," she said obediently. "Yes, thank you. I would like to marry you."

The next hour was spent walking in the garden. There were many frequent stops in which very little was said out loud. It was only when Mavis noticed that it had become rather cloudy that they became aware of the passing time.

"You have to come in for tea," Mavis insisted.

Julian needed very little convincing. He was not at all eager to rush back to the Winfields' house.

Robin was tired of waiting. He had sat by the stream for several hours now and he was tired and hungry. Finally he got his horse and left for town. There seemed to be little likelihood that Kitty would come today.

Kitty. How he wished she were here. He'd like to hold her close and tell her that he'd love her and cherish her. They could live in the country, or the city, whatever she wanted. He'd marry her even if she had no money and there had been no contract. He almost wished that there were no fortune. Then they'd be forced to live at Scotney Park, and he wouldn't have to share her with others in a series of parties and dances.

As he neared town, it began to rain.

Mavis and Julian settled themselves in the drawing room. There was no one else around, so Mavis ordered tea for the two of them. Julian marveled at his good fortune. Not only was he getting the money he needed to pay his debts, but he was getting a very pleasant wife, also. He watched her as she bustled around the tea tray, fixing his tea. He had never seen someone's appearance change so much just because of happiness. Mavis fairly radiated with it. Every once in a while, when she thought Julian wasn't looking, she watched him and wondered why he wanted to marry her.

But she was so excited that she no longer cared to look for answers.

"I have a small home in the country, in Essex," he told her. "It's not as big as this house, but it is pleasantly situated. It'll need a lot of fixing up, because I haven't spent much time there in the past few years." He took a drink of his tea.

Mavis was thrilled with the idea of being able to redecorate their home. "Do you think I can do it?" she asked. "I don't know much about furniture and wallpaper and those things."

"We'll get lots of people in to advise you. All you have to do is decide what things you like best."

She smiled at the idea of choosing colors, deciding there would be no lavender or gray in her new home. They were so agreeably engrossed in their discussion that neither of them heard William come in.

"What's he doing here?" William bellowed as he entered the drawing room and saw Julian.

Julian stood up to greet William. He had not expected a warm welcome, but he hadn't expected this either. He turned slightly to Mavis and saw that she had lost most of her radiance. She had shrunk into her chair and was looking quite worried.

"Good afternoon, Mr. Tolbert," Julian said, extending his hand.

William ignored him and strode over to Mavis. Standing directly in front of her, he demanded once more, "What's he doing here?"

Mavis tried to remain calm, but she kept remembering the awful battles that she had been in the middle of when she had considered marrying Michael. She couldn't see how anyone could object to Sir Julian, but with William one was never sure.

"He came to see me," Mavis told him.

"He came to see you?" The way he asked the question brought back all her former doubts. "Why would he come to see you?"

Julian did not know what William's point was, but he tried to intervene. "I think you should know . . ." he began.

"I don't need to hear anything from you," William yelled at Julian, "but I think there are a few things that she"—he pointed at Mavis—"should hear from me." He gave Julian a long look, and Julian stepped back to where he had been, noticing that they seemed to have gathered an audience.

Kitty had decided to come down for tea and entered the room at the same time as Alicia, who had just come in from her ride. They both stood near the door, watching their father in astonishment. Nellie joined them, still in her cloak, which was dripping with rain. She had been at the Winfields' and had come straight in when she heard the commotion.

William looked at Mavis. "Do you know what he is?" he asked, pointing at Julian. Mavis got very white. Was William going to tell her that Julian was already married? Was he going to forbid her to see him again? Julian was getting angrier by the minute. Why was her brother interfering? What gave him the right to make Mavis unhappy all the time? He felt a strong desire to take Mavis and leave.

"Do you know?" William repeated.

"What is he?" whispered Mavis, who really did not want to know.

"He's nothing but a fortune hunter, a lousy fortune hunter. . . . I found out that he has stacks of debts in London, and everybody knows that he's on the lookout for a rich wife."

Julian did not think that Mavis looked too concerned.

"Then why would he want to marry me?" Mavis laughed, much relieved. Was this William's big announcement? "I don't have any fortune." She turned to smile at Julian, but the smile froze on her face.

Julian was now as white as she had been. "But . . ." he started to say, only to stop. He couldn't very well ask her why he was told that she had lots of money if she didn't. He sat down rather heavily in the chair behind him, looking dazed.

Mavis stood up, feeling that she had abruptly strayed from a pleasant dream into a nightmare. How silly she had been in hoping for things that she should have known would never come true! Why had she ignored the question she kept asking herself—why someone like Julian would want to marry her? She had been carried away by her own silly emotions. Now all she had left was her pride, and she was determined not to give that up.

"I see," she said. Julian still had not spoken. He must have somehow believed that she had money. Everything that had followed was merely his way of convincing her that he cared about her. And she had believed him like a silly schoolgirl.

William started to speak, but Mavis glared at him. "You've said enough, I think," she said to her brother. He sat down, quite pleased with himself. He had exposed the cad; let Mavis get rid of him.

"I don't know why you thought I had a fortune," she told Julian quite calmly. "Outside of William, Kitty is the only one in the family with a real fortune. Of course, she is called Miss Tolbert also, so maybe you confused us."

Julian looked up at her, wondering at her calmness. Didn't she care at all? Yes, he could see in her eyes that she cared, a great deal. Her hands were tightly clenched, but he could see how they were shaking. He had seen her dowdy and plain, hurt and humiliated, and ecstatically happy, but he had never seen her looking so beautiful, or trying to be so brave. He stood up. The money suddenly made no difference. It was Mavis that he wanted.

"You'd better go," William growled at him.

"Mavis," Julian said, as William moved closer to him. "Please hear me out."

"You've got nothing to say to her," William said. He grabbed his arm and tried to pull him toward the door.

Julian shrugged his hand off and went back to Mavis's side. "Let me explain things to you," he pleaded, taking her hand.

She looked up at him, and Julian knew then that he really loved her. He was not going to let her brother or anyone hurt her again.

"We're going for a walk," he told William.

"Mavis, don't you go with him," William shouted after her. "I warned you about him."

Julian was leading Mavis to the door. He had a firm hold on her elbow and was not letting go.

"You can't go out there," William said. "It's raining. . . . Mavis, make him go." William was turning very red—why wouldn't she listen to him, damn her anyway?

Kitty grabbed Nellie's cloak, which was dripping on the floor, and threw it over Mavis's shoulders. It wasn't really long enough, but it would keep off most of the rain. Julian smiled gratefully at her, but Mavis hadn't even seemed to have noticed them. She was trying hard to retain her composure.

"You'll be sorry," William shouted after them, but no one was listening.

Julian led Mavis quickly into the shelter of the trees. He turned her to face him.

"Your brother told the truth," Julian said quietly. "I do have a great many debts in London, and I was looking for a rich wife. Someone had mentioned to me that there was an heiress down here, by the name of Tolbert, and I came down to try my luck with her. When I met you I thought you were the heiress. Everything seemed to go as planned except that I fell in love with you."

Mavis was determined not to believe his lies

again, and she said nothing; but Julian was encouraged by the fact that she was still listening to him.

"I really do care about you, Mavis. I couldn't bear to see your brother hurting you, and I realized that the money doesn't matter to me." He reached out and held her by the shoulders. "I still want to marry you."

Mavis pulled away from him and walked over to a nearby bush. With her back to him, she absentmindedly began to pull at the leaves. "I fear I may have been hasty earlier this afternoon when I accepted your proposal. We know so little of each other, and I think I am too set in my ways to change. I don't really feel that we are well suited."

"Oh, stop it," he shouted, striding over to where she was standing and angrily turning her around. "The only way I'll let you back out of our engagement is if you don't love me. . . . Can you look me in the face and tell me that you don't love me?"

Mavis tried to pull away from him but his eyes held her firmly. Finally she looked down and studied his coat buttons. "You have no right to ask me that," she protested. "A gentleman wouldn't pry like that."

"Don't you see, Mavis, that that's the only thing that does matter? If you love me, we can make it." Julian lifted her chin, so she looked up into his face. "Do you love me?"

She nodded slowly. "Yes," she whispered. "I do."

Julian pulled her close in his arms. "I can't offer you much," he told her, "but I do love you, and I will do all that I can to make you happy." When she didn't answer, he asked, "You do believe me, don't you?"

"Yes, I believe you," she said.

"I'll need some time," he told her. "I'll have to raise some money to pay off the debts. I have a few things that I can sell, but it'll leave me pretty well done up. The next few years may be pretty quiet and humdrum."

"No," Mavis declared. "That was how my life was up to this point. With you it can never be that way again."

Julian responded very pleasantly to her belief in him. It was a few minutes before they got back to the problem at hand.

"I could sell my house in Bath," Mavis offered. "It wouldn't bring in a lot, but it might be enough to pay off what you owe."

Much to Mavis's surprise, Julian refused her offer very firmly. It seemed strange to her that someone who was planning on marrying a woman for her money would object to taking the proceeds from her house to pay his debts.

"You can sell it, if you want," Julian told her, "but I won't take any of the money. You could invest it or get something for yourself, but I will take care of my own debts.

"I think it's about time I was responsible for myself," he continued. "I mean, if I plan to take on the responsibility of a wife, and maybe a family"—he paused to kiss a rather scarlet face pressed against his shoulder—"I ought to start by cleaning up the remnants of my past." He looked down at

Mavis. "I'm not sure how quickly I can get things settled. I may be gone several days or even weeks. Do you really believe that I will come back to you?"

"Yes," Mavis smiled, "but if you take too long, I may come after you."

"The important thing is that you remember I love you. You mustn't let your brother turn you against me."

Mavis pulled abruptly away from him. "You speak a great deal about my believing and trusting you, but you must not trust me much, to even suggest that such a thing could happen. Do you think my love for you is such a flimsy thing that I could be talked out of it?" She stood in front of him, her hands on her hips and her eyes blazing, ready to do battle. Julian just laughed and pulled her back into his arms. He held her so tightly that she could hardly breathe.

"Now that I've found you, I'm afraid that I'll lose you," he told her. "I could see what your brother was doing to you earlier, and I'm afraid that he might do it again. Only I won't be there to convince you he's wrong."

"William's words did nothing to my love for you," Mavis insisted. "They only made me unsure of your motives."

"Only! Well, don't let that happen again, do you understand?" He was suddenly very serious. "You don't doubt them now, do you? You do know that I really love you?"

"Yes, I know," she told him. "I won't doubt you again."

Reassured, Julian spent some time reminding her of his love for her.

"I'd better go," he said reluctantly. "I'll be back as soon as possible." He kissed her gently once more.

"I'll go back by myself," Mavis told him. He nodded and turned to go to the stables. At the bend in the path, he turned, raised his hand briefly, and then was gone.

Mavis sighed and walked slowly back to the house. She was surprised at how very much alone she suddenly felt.

CHAPTER ELEVEN

Robin rose early the next day, determined that he would see Kitty and tell her of his interview with her father. After fidgeting around the inn for an hour, he started out for the Tolberts'. He knew it was too early for a social call, but he hoped he might meet Kitty accidentally if she went out riding.

Crofton Grange lay close to the public road. When he was in sight of the house, he stopped his horse and peered through the trees. There was no activity to be seen, certainly no one riding away from the stables. He was disappointed, but he had to remind himself that she might not go riding today or might be in the company of her sisters. He resolutely banished such melancholy thoughts from his mind and continued down the road. He would wait where he had yesterday and hope that Kitty would ride that way.

Kitty couldn't wait to get out of the house. Her father had refused to speak to any of them the night before. So they ate dinner in silence, while William glared at them all. He said nothing of his talk with Robin. He was so angry with Mavis that he had actually forgotten about it, but Kitty assumed that he would eventually get around to telling her that she was no longer betrothed to Lord Scotney.

Kitty had managed to avoid Nellie last night, because she couldn't bear to hear how, because of their efforts, Lord Scotney could now marry his "true love." Nellie was so full of the romance of it all that she never noticed that her sister didn't share her excitement and was not quite thrilled about reuniting the parted lovers.

With the news of Mavis's engagement, it had not been hard to keep the conversation in safe areas, but this morning it might not be so easy. So Kitty decided to slip out of the house early and try to talk herself into a more cheerful mood. How she would do this she had no idea, but she had resolved to get Robin out of her system.

After a quick breakfast, she went out to the stables, had her horse saddled for her, and rode off.

She let her horse choose the way, inattentively noting the path they took. Suddenly she awoke from her daydream and realized that they were heading toward the stream where she had first met Robin. Kitty started to turn her horse to go elsewhere, but then decided not to leave. Maybe it was best to go to a place that was special to her.

Her horse reached the old wall and began to graze, so she slipped off her back. She led her over to the stream and tied her loosely to a branch so the horse could move around a little. She walked slowly around the area, stopping occasionally as she remembered their first meeting. When she came to the spot near the wall where she had fallen into the bushes, Kitty noticed that she was crying. This is hardly the way to forget all about Robin, she scolded herself. But it was easier to cry than not to, so she gave in to the impulse, assuring herself that all she needed was one good cry, then she'd really get herself under control.

As Robin came along the path from the road, he thought that he heard the sound of crying. He hurried his horse along, and soon he saw a very forlorn Kitty, sitting huddled by the wall, crying into a very inadequate square of linen.

"What's wrong? Are you hurt?" he asked, rushing over to her side.

Seeing Robin looking so concerned made her want to cry even harder, but that would accomplish nothing. So she made herself slow down the flow of tears and try to answer him. "No," she sniffed, "I'm just fine."

Robin looked down at her dejectedly for a moment, thinking of his broken promise to her. "I know why you're crying," he told her quietly.

"You do?" Kitty was considerably startled. How could he know that she was in love with him? She stopped crying and looked at him in apprehension.

"I tried, Kitty, I really did." Robin got up, walked a little way away from her, and tied his horse to a low bush. Then he continued, "I know it doesn't help any, but I'm truly sorry. I wish it could have been different, but it seems it can't." He came back to where she was still sitting.

Kitty was thoroughly confused. It seemed that he did know that she loved him, but how could he have found out? Would Nellie have told him? No, he didn't seem to have known yesterday when he spoke to her. Well, thought Kitty, she was not interested in his pity, and he didn't need to put on such an act of sympathy. She stood up slowly and tried to look dignified.

"I'm afraid I don't know what you are talking about," she told him haughtily, and started back to where her horse was tied.

He reached out and stopped her before she got very far.

"I know, Kitty. You don't have to pretend with me. Nellie told me," he said.

"Just what did Nellie tell you?" Kitty demanded, still retaining her cool composure.

"About Edward," he said simply.

Kitty forgot about her dignity as she lost herself in confusion.

"Edward?" she asked cautiously.

Robin pulled her over to a fallen tree that was in the shade. She sat down reluctantly. She knew she would be better off not staying, but she was curious to learn what he was talking about.

"She told me how you met him, how you fell in love, and how your father won't even let him come to see you." Noticing how still Kitty was, he hastened to reassure her. "I shouldn't pry into something that isn't my business, but I'm glad that she told me."

Part of Kitty was admiring Nellie's ingenuity—it was a good story to convince Robin that he shouldn't marry her—but the rest of her was indignant that he could believe that she was in love with someone else.

"Have you told him yet?" Robin asked.

"Told who what?" Kitty had not been paying attention.

"Have you told Edward that you have to marry me?"

Kitty was so confused that she could just stare at him. She had thought that the object of Nellie's story was to make Robin unwilling to marry her, so why was he talking as if the wedding was still going to take place?

"No, I haven't told him," Kitty said, thinking that she could hardly tell something to someone who didn't even exist.

Robin was playing with a stick he had picked up. "I really did try," he said, not watching her, "but your father was so set on the idea of our marrying that he wouldn't budge."

Oh, thought Kitty, finally something makes sense. He doesn't know that I love him, he was upset because Father refused to let him out of the contract. Kitty remembered—just in time to lower her rapidly rising spirits—that Robin was really in love with someone else and wanted only a marriage of convenience. The thought of that lady stopped her for a minute, but not for long. I did what I could to get him free, she thought, but Father just won't cooperate.

"I know it's not what you wanted," Robin was saying, "but I'll try to help you forget him." He got up and walked a few feet away from her. "It may not be the right thing to mention just now, but I won't make any demands on you . . . after we're married . . . not until you're ready."

Kitty just stared at him in dismay. Just what kind of demands was he willing not to make? Did he mean he would not demand her time, her attention, or her love, or that he was in no hurry to make physical demands of her? It seemed that a marriage of convenience was what he wanted, after all. Would that sort of arrangement be better than never seeing him at all? Kitty didn't see that she had any real choice, because her father had already refused to break the contract. Kitty wondered if she had any chance of winning Robin's love after they were married. She sensed that if she wanted that, and she readily admitted that she did, she must be careful not to be too possessive of him now. She must convince him that she would try very hard to adjust to a marriage of convenience.

He came back to where she was sitting. He seemed embarrassed by what he had said. "I mean, I know you are in love with someone else and you would not welcome my attentions."

Would that really be true? Kitty wondered. She thought it might be, for she certainly would not welcome advances from someone other than Robin. Well, first she would have to get Edward out of the picture.

"I fear you may have gotten the wrong idea about Edward and me," she told him nervously. "Nellie does tend to exaggerate things." She hesitated, trying to decide how her story should proceed, but Robin thought it was because the subject was upsetting her.

"You don't have to talk about it if it is too painful for you," he said.

Kitty was about to confess the truth to him, but he was being so sympathetic that she felt she couldn't. She feared he would be awfully angry.

"I think you should know the truth," Kitty said, trying to sound brave. "You see, Edward was not exactly an honorable man. . . . I was very trusting when I met him and believed everything that he told me." She was picking up speed as the story developed in her mind. "He pretended to love me, but all he wanted was my money." Kitty noticed that Robin looked a bit grim; perhaps she shouldn't have mentioned the money. She hastened to point out the differences in the two cases. "He kept telling me that the money did not make any difference, that he had fallen in love with me before he had even known that I had any money. At first I believed him, but he made little mistakes, and soon I realized that he had been lying to me all along. The only reason that he had been friendly and complimentary was to win my love, and my money.

"I had written to Nellie several times while I was in Brighton, and I must have mentioned him occasionally. I guess that she got the wrong idea, because I never did tell her the truth. I was too ashamed of how foolish I had been in trusting him." She smiled encouragingly at Robin. "You've always been honest with me," she told him. "I have always known that you were here because of the contract, that money was the only reason that we would marry. You have never tried to disguise your motives by pretending to care for me; in fact, you have been truthful enough to admit that you are in love with someone else." She got up and began to walk along the wall.

Good Lord, thought Robin, I've really got myself into a box now. Why did he ever make that stupid comment about being in love with someone other than his intended wife? It had caused him nothing but trouble. He watched Kitty as she walked slowly away from him. The more he saw of her, the more deeply in love he found himself. He was constantly making resolutions to tell her of his feelings, but now he really couldn't. After her encounter with the dishonorable Edward, she would think he was lying to hide the fact that her main attraction was her money—especially because she believed that he was in love with someone else. Even to him, the truth sounded pretty weak. He sighed as he got up and walked over to her. Well, at least she wasn't in love with Edward.

Kitty turned around as Robin neared her. She had been pleased with her little tale. She had eliminated Edward as a former love and had also acknowledged the fact that Robin was marrying her because of her money, not because of love. There were only a few extra points she hoped to throw in.

She looked at Robin. He didn't look quite as cheered by her honesty as she had hoped. Of course, he wasn't getting the woman he loved, so he had little reason to be happy.

"I hope my honesty did not offend you," she said. "I only wanted you to know that I am aware of the kind of marriage that you want, and I am willing to try not to interfere with you after the wedding." She started to pick some of the wildflowers that grew along the wall so she could avoid looking at him. "I might not be very good at it," she told him candidly. "But if you tell me when you don't want me around or when something is none of my affair, I'll try to cooperate."

Robin took the flowers out of her hand, and turned her around to face him. He might not feel that the time was right to tell her he loved her, but he could clear up this nonsense about a marriage of convenience.

"That's not the kind of marriage that I want," he told her. "Alicia doesn't know everything. Not everyone wants that kind of marriage. I realize that we started off badly and that you are probably wary of giving your affections again, but I would hope, after we are married, that that would change. I do like you, and we seem to get along well. I think it could be the basis for a very comfortable marriage. . . . I'm not in the habit of traveling much, but if you wanted to visit the fashionable spots, we could. And spend the season in London, too. . . . I would like us to be friends if we could. . . . Maybe, after a while, a certain degree of affection would grow. . . . It might not be the ideal marriage, but it would definitely not be a marriage of convenience." He looked at Kitty. She had not said much.

"You weren't planning on having a lot of married women or widows around?" she asked him quietly.

"No," he assured her, "I think I'll have my hands full just having you around."

"I'm glad," Kitty said, smiling shyly at him. She did not entirely understand that last part, so she ignored it.

Robin took her hand. "You don't mind marrying me?" he asked her.

"No," she said. "I think I'd like to."

She smiled at him so delightfully that Robin was hard put not to pull her into his arms and kiss her. But because he was trying for friendship first, he felt it might be pushing his luck just a bit too far. He kissed her hand instead.

"Friends?" he asked.

She nodded happily, and he relinquished her hand. They walked in silence over to where her horse was grazing. He untied it for her.

"I'll come over later today to tell your father that it's all settled," he told her. "He will probably want to set a definite date, so you'd better think about how soon you want to be a married lady."

In spite of his earlier decision, Robin leaned over and kissed her gently on the lips. She didn't seem at all upset by the slight change in their relationship. Robin hoped he might be able to tell her of his love before too long.

He lifted her up into the saddle, and she started off toward her home, stopping once to wave goodbye.

Kitty was in a very happy mood when she returned home. She hadn't forgotten about the woman whom Robin loved, but he had said he liked her and was willing to marry her. The best thing was that he didn't want a marriage of convenience. Maybe, someday, he would fall in love with her, and then everything would be perfect.

She left Dancer in the stables and walked to the house in a dreamworld. She was quite surprised when her father greeted her in the hallway. He wasn't usually home at this time of the day.

"Kitty," he called, "I want to talk to you . . . in here." He opened the library door.

She entered it after her father and was surprised to see a strange woman sitting there. She was sitting near the wall in a straight-backed chair that few people ever used. It was a measure of someone's social standing where her father had them sit. Those chairs near the wall were reserved for people who were not really welcome in the house, but who were there for some reason.

The woman stood up as they entered, but William made no effort to introduce them. Instead he led Kitty over to the sofa by the fireplace. He sat down next to her and took one of her hands.

"You know, Kitty, that I've always said that you had to marry Lord Scotney," he began. "I've always known that you were against the idea, but I always told you that I knew best. . . . Even when it turned out that you were going to marry Claude's brother, whom we had never met, I still refused to drop the idea. I wouldn't even listen when you pointed out that we knew nothing about him and it was unfair to make you marry him."

"But it's all right, Father," Kitty interrupted. "I don't mind. . . . He seems very nice." It wasn't like her father to suddenly consider her feelings, not when he was so set on his own way.

William seemed very ill at ease. "It's good of you to try to make me feel better because you know how much I wanted this wedding, but it seems you were right, after all."

Kitty looked at him in surprise. He stood up and drew her over to the side of the room. The woman stood up and Kitty got a better look at her.

She was a tall woman, with bright red hair. Her clothes were cheaply made and not in good taste. Her dress was a bright green and more suited to a ballroom than a morning social call. It was cut low and exposed far more of her breasts than Kitty would have thought acceptable. What surprised Kitty most was the way that this woman was looking at her. It was a look of pure loathing, as if she had caught Kitty trying to steal something of hers. Kitty moved closer to her father.

"Kitty," he said, "this is the Countess of Scotney."

Kitty looked at her father. This woman was certainly too young to be Robin's mother, but what else could her father mean?

"She is Lord Scotney's wife," he said.

Kitty turned toward the woman, almost expecting to see some sign that would contradict her father's words. Robin couldn't be married. He wouldn't have said all those things to her if he had been.

"That's right, sweetie," the woman said proudly.

Kitty turned to her father.

"Is it true?" she asked him.

Before he could answer, the door opened. A maid came in carrying a baby. Kitty's face must have shown the surprise she felt, because the woman said, "That's our son." She went over and took the child from the maid's arms.

Kitty went over to see the child, almost against her will. She pulled the thin blanket back from his head. There was a little face looking back at her, with Robin's dark brown hair covering his head and his solemn blue eyes watched her steadily.

"How old is he?" Kitty asked.

"He's almost a year," the woman said. She looked at William, who said nothing, so she began to explain to Kitty. "I used to work for Lord Scotney's father, and Robin"—she looked knowingly at Kitty—"well, he was always after me. I was all alone. I didn't have anybody to protect me; besides, he promised to marry me. When I was going to have the baby, he tried to ignore me. Said it wasn't his, but he knew it was. Finally his father found out about it and made him marry me. He don't come to see us much, but we're married all right." She shifted the child in her arms. "I guess all your money was a bit too tempting for him to pass up, but I couldn't let him do it. Now that his pa and brother are dead, I'm the Countess. He's going to have to admit it. If he got himself involved with you there'd be a scandal, and I might never be accepted. . . . I've got my rights, you know." Her eyes softened when she saw Kitty's real distress. "It's better this way," she said. "He's no good. . . . He'd only make you unhappy. You'll do much better without him."

Mr. Tolbert moved to the door. "I think you'd better go now. Your husband's at an inn in town, if you want to see him," he said. "If you had hoped to get some money from me, you were wrong."

"I don't want your money," she told him coldly. "I came here to protect my rights and my son's." She turned to the door. "Good day," she said, then left.

Kitty was shaking so hard that her father had to lead her to a chair.

"Is it really true?" she asked again.

"How should I know?" he demanded. He was worried that this story might get out and make him the butt of all kinds of jokes. He turned back to Kitty, and he momentarily forgot his anger when he saw how pale she was. He got her a glass of water with a few drops of brandy in it.

William brought the glass over and made Kitty swallow some, then he went on. "She had some papers and they looked legal to me, but I couldn't tell for sure. She claimed they were married in Scotland, and they write up the marriage lines differently there. She wouldn't let me keep them. . . . Sounded like he had tried to destroy the papers so he could be rid of her. She isn't exactly the kind of woman you want for a Countess."

Kitty seemed a little better, so he continued to expound. "I'm really shocked that he would still come here when he knew he couldn't marry you. Well," he said, as he stood up, "there's no denying the man's a real louse, but I'll admit that I'm disappointed that you won't be a Countess. I was really hoping for that."

Together they walked toward the door. Kitty seemed to have recovered from her initial shock. "You're lucky to be out of it," he told her. "Though he seemed like a decent fellow. Hard to believe that he could have fooled us all."

"But I don't think he did, Father," Kitty said.

William stopped and stared at her. "What do you mean?"

"I mean that I don't believe that that woman is his wife. I don't think that he would have come if he was already married. He didn't talk as if he was married." She was annoyed to find herself blushing.

William watched her blush, with displeasure. "Oh, he didn't, did he? Just how do unmarried men talk?" He went on before Kitty could answer, assuming that she would have. "I don't care what you think. I saw the papers and the child, and that woman said things to me that convinced me that she was telling the truth." Any doubts that he had had in the matter disappeared in the face of Kitty's hesitations.

"Maybe she was only his mistress," Kitty suggested.

"And you think that's all right then?" William asked. He had branded Robin a smooth-talking devil and was angry with Kitty's defense of him.

"Well, the least you could do," Kitty persisted, "would be to ask him if it's true. That woman could have been lying, you know."

"Why? She didn't ask for anything," he said. "You're just besotted with the first handsome man who paid a little attention to you. I made a mistake in arranging a marriage with someone I didn't know, and I've admitted it; so let's be done with it all. I'll not have that man in my house again." He stopped for a moment and tried to calm himself down. "You were attracted to him. I know that, Kitty. But don't try to fool yourself into believing it was all a lie. That woman had no reason to make up the story. She wasn't asking for money or anything. She just wanted her rightful place in society. He's a scoundrel. A smooth-talking one, but still a scoundrel. He got you to believe just what he wanted you to believe."

William's quieter tone was more persuasive than his belligerence. Whereas she could argue with his earlier statements, she found it hard to argue with his quiet logic. What did she actually know about Robin, except what he had told her?

When Robin arrived at the Tolberts' he was surprised that he was not shown into a room to wait but was left just inside the front door. He was even more surprised when William came storming out of the library and charged down the hall toward him. William had not been this angry yesterday, when Robin last saw him. He assumed something else must have caused this.

"You have a lot of nerve coming here again," William shouted at Robin, who was only a few feet away by this time.

"I'm sorry if I upset you yesterday," Robin said, "but Kitty and I have worked out our difficulties, and we are no longer opposed to the wedding."

"You stay away from my daughter, you hear?" William was shouting loud enough for the whole house to hear him. "If you come near her again, I'll have you thrashed." He was bearing down on Robin, who, in turn, was backing toward the door. "She doesn't know how to deal with a womanizer like you, but I do."

"What are you talking about?" Robin asked, trying very hard to remain courteous. "I'm no womanizer. I've led a very quiet life. I'm not going to hurt Kitty. I just want to know what you're talking about."

By this time William had backed him right out the door, so Robin was standing outside. "We know the truth about you now, so go back to town. Go where you want, but don't come back here. You aren't welcome here. Ever. The marriage is off."

As William slammed the door, Robin thought he heard Kitty calling his name; but he could not get anyone to let him in again. He started to walk around the side of the house, but a very large footman came out and told him to leave. There wasn't much that he could do but obey. He remounted and headed back to the inn, wondering what had been going on.

Kitty was sitting at her window seat, watching as a gentle breeze blew the branches of the trees. She wondered if the child was really his son. There were resemblances, but it was very hard to tell with a child that young. It was the child that upset her most, she realized. She was not so sheltered that she wasn't aware that many men had mistresses before they were married, and very often they had children by them. It was an easy fact to accept when it was just a general statement about people you didn't know, but when it concerned someone you had met, someone you were fond of, it was much harder.

Kitty felt that the woman had chosen her way of life, but the child did not ask to be born. It was not quite so easy to abandon him to a life of poverty. If the woman were Robin's mistress and not his wife, Kitty knew that she would face a very difficult decision. Could she marry him, assuming her father relented, and ignore the child's existence? Even to provide for him didn't seem enough, for it would not give him his father's love and companionship. She just didn't know what she could do.

She was roused from her thoughts by the sound of yelling downstairs. She could hear no other voice but her father's, but he must have been talking to Robin. Who else would he be saying such things to?

Kitty jumped to her feet and flew out of her room. She was halfway down the stairs when she saw her father slamming the door.

"Robin!" she screamed, but the door had closed. She ran down the rest of the stairs and across the hall. When she reached the door, she tugged at the handle, trying to pull it open; but her father dragged her away.

"What are you doing?" he yelled at her. "Are you planning to throw yourself at him, like some cheap shopgirl? Haven't you got any pride?" He suddenly remembered where he was and pulled her into the nearest room, away from the interested ears of the staff.

"Why didn't you ask him the truth?" Kitty screamed at him, before he had a chance to speak. "You never asked him, did you?"

"I don't need his explanation," William shouted back. "I know him for what he is now, and I don't want any more to do with him." He said more quietly, "Look at the grief he's caused you. Is that what you want the rest of your life to be like?"

He tried to reason with her. "He's just not good enough for you, Kitty. Let him go; find someone who'll care about you, not just want you for your money like he did."

Kitty would not listen to his arguments, no matter how persuasive they might be.

"Couldn't you have asked him anyway? You have taken the word of some strange woman, whom you never met before, and believed it. You could have asked him if it was true."

William detected a note of hysteria in her voice, and he was worried. Was she really attracted to this man?

"All right," he agreed. "I'm going to town in a

little while. I'll stop at the inn and talk to him."

"I'm coming, too," Kitty said. "I want to hear what he has to say."

"No." William was firm. "I'll go, but you're staying here. If you won't agree to that, then I won't go and talk to him. It's this way, or not at all."

Kitty was not really left much choice. "All right," she said. "But you have to be fair. Give him a chance to explain."

"I will," he promised, anxious to alleviate her concern. He was not about to let Kitty marry this man, but maybe she needed to have him admit the truth before she could believe it herself. William was not worried, though. He was convinced that they had already heard the truth. All Lord Scotney could do was confirm it.

CHAPTER TWELVE

Robin had had no idea what Mr. Tolbert had been talking about, and he returned to the inn thoroughly puzzled.

He changed his clothing while his luncheon was being prepared. He ate, scarcely noticing what he was eating. As he finished, the innkeeper remembered that there was a young lady waiting to see him. Robin mentally cursed him for not telling him sooner, for he was sure that it was Kitty waiting for him. He burst into the parlor, only to find a strange woman waiting there.

"You Robin Prentice?" she asked.

He nodded.

"I'm Daisy Abbot," she said. She stopped to change the position of a bundle in her lap, and Robin saw that she had a child with her. "I was hired by a friend of yours . . . Sir Matthew Trilby."

"That's nice," he said, wondering what all this had to do with him.

"I'm an actress, and I don't usually take on this kind of work; but he said you'd pay well."

Robin felt that he was wasting his time and wondered how he could get away. "What kind of work?" he asked. He was not in the mood for any of Trilby's jokes.

"Don't try to make out like you don't know anything about this," she yelled at him. The ladylike facade was rapidly slipping. "I was hired to do a simple job. I did it and I want my money."

Robin tried to quiet her. "Just tell me what Trilby asked you to do, and I'll pay you," he assured her. "I just didn't know that he was going to hire you." He motioned for her to sit down and then did likewise.

"I was hired to be your wife," she said. "Tom, here, he's supposed to be your son."

"You were what?" Robin jumped up. What was this now? "Who were you supposed to pretend this for?" he asked, almost sure of the answer.

"He said it was to get you out of an engagement you didn't want to be in." Daisy was getting a little impatient. This man was acting as though he had never heard of the idea. He'd better not try to weasel out of paying her, or he'd find himself in real trouble.

"You went to the Tolberts' house?" he asked in a tight voice.

"Yeah," she said. "That was the name."

Robin sat down again and put his head in his hands. So this was what Mr. Tolbert was so upset about, and no wonder. Who would want his daughter to marry a man who already had a wife and child?

"I think you'd better tell me everything that you did," he said. He had a sinking feeling that he was not going to like what he heard.

"You gonna pay me?" she asked.

"Yes, I'll pay you."

"Just wanted to make sure," she said. "A girl has the right to get paid, you know." He nodded warily. "Well, let's see." She settled herself in her chair. "I went to the Tolberts', like I was told. I saw a Mr. Tolbert first. He asked all sorts of questions about me and you and the baby. I had some fake papers that Sir Matthew had given me to use. He said they didn't look right, but I told him that we were married in Scotland, and they wrote up the marriage lines different up there. Lud," she laughed, "I thought he'd pop off, he was so angry." She spent a few minutes chuckling at the memory, while Robin silently cursed Trilby. "Then his daughter comes in. The father ignores me, and starts telling her . . . She looked kind of upset. I felt sorry for her, but I did what I was paid to do . . . or, what I'm going to be paid for doing." She looked accusingly at Robin. When he nodded again, she resumed her story.

"Tom had been crying earlier, and the old gent couldn't stand it, so he sent for some woman to look after him. After he tells his daughter about me, the woman comes back with Tom. I started to lay it on, about how you seduced me, and then your father made you marry me, and all that. I'm a good actress you know. . . . The girl, she was all white and shaky, and I wanted to make it easier for her, so I told her you were no good. . . . Then the old man orders me out. I'm sure he don't want you around there anymore either." She stopped talking to laugh at her performance.

Robin hadn't imagined a complication like this one. Why would Trilby do something like this? Then Robin remembered asking for his help before he had left London.

"I want to get paid," Daisy reminded him.

"I'll pay you," Robin insisted. "But there's more that you have to do."

She looked at him suspiciously. "I ain't like that," she said. "I'm a respectable actress."

"I'm sure you are," he said, "but you have to go

back to the Tolberts' and tell them that it was all a mistake. Tell them that you made it all up."

"Listen, I'm a real good actress," she told him. "They ain't gonna believe that I made it up. I did it too well when I was there before."

"Well," Robin got a sudden inspiration. "Tell them that it was my brother you were talking about."

She looked at him blankly while he explained, "He was supposed to marry the woman, but he died. Tell them that you didn't know that he died, but when you came here you discovered the truth."

"Why are you doing all this?" she asked. "I thought you didn't want to marry the girl. Won't this get you back with her?"

"That's the idea," Robin said. "Will you do it?"

A knock sounded at the parlor door. Robin went over to answer it as she said, "Listen, you never paid me for going to the Tolberts' and telling that story the first time. If you want me to make up another story, you'll have to pay me even more."

"Sure, sure," Robin agreed. "I'll pay you whatever you want." At this point he opened the door to a very red-faced William Tolbert.

"Well, well. Look who's here," Daisy cried. "I was just coming to see you . . ." She stopped when Robin glared at her and retreated to a corner to sulk.

"Come in, Mr. Tolbert," Robin said. As William entered, he tried to explain. "There's been a misunderstanding. This woman is not my wife."

"So I heard," William answered.

"You see, it was all a mistake," Robin continued, wondering just how much William had overheard.

"You paid her to do it," William accused.

"Not yet, he didn't," Daisy inserted, with a rather false smile. She went back to her injured silence when both Robin and William ignored her.

"I can explain, Mr. Tolbert," Robin said. "It isn't like it sounds."

"Go ahead," William said, thinking that Robin would soon be out of Kitty's life for good.

"I didn't actually hire this woman to do anything," Robin told him.

"That's right," Daisy said. "His friend did." This time Daisy returned Robin's glare. She was afraid she was not going to get paid and decided to have a bit of fun with this group instead.

"My friend thought he was doing me a favor because he felt I was reluctant to marry Kitty. I didn't know anything about it." He looked at Daisy for confirmation.

"That's right," she said. "But he's the one who was supposed to pay. He wanted me to do some more for him, too. Didn't you, sugar?" She gave Robin a suggestive look, which was intended for William's benefit.

"I see," William said. "Your friend wanted to help you get out of your engagement and hired this woman for you, to impersonate your wife."

"That's what happened," Robin admitted. William's calm surprised him.

"So even though you didn't want to marry my daughter, you led her to believe that you cared about her and encouraged her to think that you wanted this marriage as much as she did. Then you plotted to hurt her by presenting this . . . this . . . woman"—Daisy jumped up in protest at the way he said it—"as your wife."

"But I didn't know about it," Robin protested.

"It doesn't matter," William shouted. "You hurt my little girl. . . . You made her trust you, while you and your friends were plotting out this lie." He went to the door. "She begged me to come here and see you. She was convinced that you had not married her." He pointed to Daisy. "She wanted to give you a chance to defend yourself. . . . When I came here, I never dreamed that I would learn the kind of things that I have. I was wrong when I called you a womanizer, but you are indeed a scoundrel. Neither was I wrong when I said that you may not see Kitty again and that the wedding is off." He bowed toward Daisy. "Good day." Then he left.

"Kind of touchy, ain't he?" Daisy observed. She watched Robin stare in dismay at the closed door. "Say, do you still want me to go back out there again?" When he didn't answer, she shook her head. "Probably wouldn't work anyway." The baby started to cry. "Well, I need my money to get back to London."

Robin was lost in his own thoughts and did not hear Daisy.

"Say," she said again. "Can I have my money? I got other things to do, you know."

Robin looked up finally, but he didn't seem to be able to place her.

"Oh yes, your money," he remembered. He pulled out a rather thin wallet. "How much did Trilby say I'd pay you?"

She eyed him speculatively. "Twenty pounds," she said.

"Twenty pounds! I haven't got twenty pounds." He counted the money there. "The best I can do is five." He held out the bills.

She took them quickly, shrugging her shoulders. It was almost too easy—cheating this one out of his money. "Got any other jobs you want me to do?" she asked, tucking the bills down the front of her dress.

But Robin was deep in his own thoughts once more and didn't answer. Daisy looked at him, debating whether she should repeat her offer. Finally she picked up the baby and went out of the room.

"I can make more money in London, anyway," she said to herself as she closed the door.

At first Robin had been quite angry at Trilby for interfering as he did, but he had to be honest with himself. He remembered asking for Trilby's help the day that he had met with his lawyer. Even before he left London, Trilby had hinted about another plan, but Robin had not taken the trouble to find out what his friend had in mind. No, it was his own fault, Robin had to admit. He was in such a hurry to get out of the engagement that he never thought things through.

Placing the blame for the whole thing did very little to clear it up. Regardless of whose fault it was, Robin knew he'd do better to concentrate on his immediate plans.

He still wanted to marry Kitty very much, and he was not going to give up just because William told him to. He didn't much care what William thought of him if Kitty would believe him. That was the main thing. He had to make Kitty believe that he had nothing to do with Trilby's plan. He suspected that she had had plans of her own to get out of the wedding, so she ought to be understanding about this.

Robin got up and went to the window. It was only early afternoon. It seemed as though it should be much later, considering all that had happened since he saw Kitty that morning. He wondered whether he would be allowed to see Kitty if he went to the Tolberts'. He doubted it. Even if William eventually softened toward him, there hadn't been enough time for that to have happened yet. He decided, instead, to go to the creek and wait for Kitty there. If she did not come today, then he'd go there tomorrow. He'd continue to wait until he got to explain things to her. Robin left the inn to begin his vigil, feeling very hopeful.

* * *

William found Kitty waiting when he entered the house. He was not going to enjoy telling her the truth. He felt they were well rid of Lord Scotney, but, for some strange reason, Kitty seemed to be attached to him. What he had to say would hurt her, he was sure, and he hated to see her suffer any more.

"Well, did you see him?" Kitty asked as soon as he came through the door. "What did he say?"

"Let's go in here," William suggested and went into the library.

He went to look out a window, trying to buy some time. He couldn't decide the best way to tell her what had happened.

"Did you see him?" she persisted.

"Yes," William finally admitted, "I saw him." Maybe there was no good way to say it.

He turned around and went over to where she was impatiently waiting and sat down. "Kitty, I don't know why you are so suddenly interested in this man. A week ago you wouldn't even allow us to mention his name, and now you are taking up his defense. I don't understand it."

Kitty was not blind to the fact that he was not getting to the main point, and it worried her. Had she been wrong about Robin? She had been so sure that it was all a misunderstanding and hadn't even allowed herself to consider that it might be true.

"Was it true, then?" she whispered. "Was she his wife?"

"No, they weren't married, and no, she wasn't even his mistress," he added, anticipating her next question.

"Then what's wrong?" Kitty asked. "Something has upset you."

William got up and leaned against the mantel. He tried to look at Kitty but found it impossible to speak when he saw the hope in her eyes.

"Damn it, Kitty. Why are you so set on this man? Can't you just accept the fact that you're too good for him?" She was watching him steadily, as if she were daring him to try to break her faith in Robin. "Can't you see he doesn't want you?"

"That's not true," Kitty insisted, remembering their meeting earlier that morning. He had been gentle and considerate. Would he have been that way if he did not want to marry her? "Why, he even said that he liked the way that I played the pianoforte when he was here."

"That should be proof enough," William said. "Nobody likes the way you play. That shows you he was just trying to fool us."

Kitty remembered she had had similar thoughts that evening, but she still did not believe what her father was saying.

"Maybe he was just trying to be polite," she suggested.

William was losing his temper. He remembered it was impossible to reason with Kitty, but he never noticed that he was equally hard to convince.

"I suppose he was just being polite when he paid some girl to pretend to be his wife just to get out of marrying you," he shouted at her. He was so exasperated that he forgot he meant to break it to her gently.

"He did what?" Kitty asked, thoroughly astonished.

William calmed down a little before answering. "He paid an actress to come here and tell us that story."

"And the child?"

"I don't know who the child belonged to. Not to him, certainly. They probably just went out and borrowed one that had the right coloring. It was just all part of a plan to get him out of the contract."

Kitty remembered her own attempts at breaking the contract. "Maybe he planned it all a long time ago, before he came here," she said hopefully.

"Kitty, he was paying her when I got to the inn. How do you think I learned the whole story?"

"I don't believe you," Kitty shouted at her father and went to the window, turning her back on him. Actually she didn't know what to think. Robin had been so nice that morning, it didn't seem possible that he was planning such a thing. If he hadn't wanted to marry her, why couldn't he have just told her? Then she remembered that he had tried to get out of the contract before, but William had refused to let him. So what real good

227

would it have done to tell her, when William was the one whom he had to convince?

"Whatever you think, it's the truth. He was the one who admitted it to me," William told her. "But you'd rather believe him than me, wouldn't you?"

"It's all your fault anyway," Kitty accused him. "If you had let him out of the contract in the first place, he wouldn't have had to go to all these lengths to get free."

"So, now I'm the one in the wrong, is that it?" William was really angry now. He was not about to be made to look like the villain. All he had done was try to marry his daughter off, then protect her from a dishonorable man. He had not done anything wrong! "You'll apologize for that, young lady."

Kitty responded by turning her back on him, which only infuriated him more.

"Go to your room!" he demanded. "You are not leaving this house until you apologize to me."

He had expected Kitty to say she was sorry then, but she just went quietly to the door and left.

Robin was sure when it started to get dark that Kitty was not coming again that day. He had begun his wait very hopefully, but as he mounted his horse, his spirits were low indeed. He feared that Kitty had believed the worst of him and was staying close to her house to avoid him.

When he returned to the inn, he was hot, thirsty, and very depressed. He found himself a dark corner of the public room and proceeded to quench his thirst and drown his sorrows. By the time that he dragged his body up to his room, he was making complicated plans to kidnap Kitty from right under William's nose and make off with her to Scotney Park. Luckily, he fell asleep before he could carry them out.

By the middle of the next morning, Robin was once more sitting on the wall, waiting for Kitty. He had brought some food with him and was prepared to wait all day if he he had to.

By morning Kitty was quite thoroughly unhappy. The day before, she had relied on her anger toward her father to keep her from feeling too upset. But she couldn't bring her anger back in the morning.

The whole house was empty when Kitty got downstairs. It was very late for breakfast, and the food was cold. The cook offered to make something fresh for her, but Kitty didn't think it was worth the trouble. She just wasn't hungry. She went off in search of Nellie, or anybody, but she seemed to have been deserted.

She could see Mavis walking in the garden, and Nellie and Alicia were probably out riding. Since she was forbidden to leave the house, both of these activities were denied her. Eventually, she wandered into the library and chose a book to read.

Mavis was trying very hard to keep busy. It was only two days now since Julian had left, but it seemed like years. She was careful to appear cheerful and confident when William was around, because he seemed to be just waiting for her faith in Julian to slip. During the day, she found all sorts of tasks to keep her busy, but Julian still managed to creep into her thoughts.

After breakfast, she decided to go out and pick some flowers. This was a pleasant thing to do when she began to feel low, because she had some very nice memories that took place in the garden. Unfortunately, the one thing the house did not need was more cut flowers. There were arrangements in every space imaginable, and since Mavis had cut most of those yesterday, they didn't really need replacing yet.

Mavis reached the part of the garden where Julian had asked her if she was going to the assembly. She remembered seeing him walking along the paths, coming toward her. She wandered slowly along, not picking much, when the sound of a horse broke into her thoughts.

She looked down to the drive and saw a man dismounting, while a groom stood by, ready to take his horse. She wondered if until Julian returned she was going to think everybody looked like him. As the man came toward the gardens, she realized that it looked like Julian because that's who it was. She immediately forgot all her years of training in ladylike behavior.

"Julian!" she cried happily.

She dropped the basket of flowers and the shears and ran down the path. Julian had stopped at the sound of her voice and looked to see where she was. When he saw her coming down the path, he went forward to meet her. They met near a bend in the path, which hid them from the curious eyes of the groom.

Mavis stopped a few feet away from him, suddenly realizing how her behavior must look. The years of uncertainty and no self-confidence came rushing back. Maybe he had come to tell her that he didn't want to marry her after all. She watched him fearfully. He seemed to be able to read her thoughts and know just what she was feeling. He smiled slowly and held out his arms. She threw herself into them.

"Oh, Julian. It's been so long," she scolded him. When he started to laugh, she blushed. "I know its only been a few days, but it seemed long."

"I have the feeling you were wondering whether I was really coming back. Weren't you?" he teased.

"I was not," Mavis denied. "I was just impatient to see you again."

He laughed and bent his head to kiss her. She had lost her shyness and reached up eagerly to meet his lips. As he kissed her, all her doubts slipped away, and she forgot that she had ever had them.

"Well, what have you been doing since I left you?" he asked, as they strolled back up the path.

"Picking flowers mostly," Mavis laughed. They had reached her basket, and Julian helped her pick up her things. "For the library, the drawing room, the dining room, for everyone's bedroom, and then some more for the library and the drawing room."

"I doubt that you need this one, then," he said, holding up a flower that had been stepped on in her rush to meet him.

Mavis shook her head. "We didn't need any of them. It just kept me busy."

"Too busy to think of me at all?" he asked.

"Oh, I thought of you a few times," she teased.

"Just a few times, was it?" he asked. He moved very close and put his arms around her. "So you only thought of me a few times, while I was thinking of you every minute. Just how many times is a few?" He leaned over and kissed the white skin of her neck. As his lips moved along her skin, she found it increasingly difficult to think coherently.

"A few million, maybe," she whispered.

"Ah, that's better," he said, as his lips found hers once more.

After a few minutes, they moved on to a bench in a small clearing. Mavis put her basket on the ground as they settled themselves on the seat.

"How has your brother been?" Julian asked.

"I'm not sure, because he doesn't speak to me anymore."

Julian looked at her seriously. "I never wanted to come between you and your brother, Mavis. I hope that he will learn to accept me once we're married." He moved closer to her. "Does it bother you that he doesn't think you should marry me?"

"No," Mavis shook her head. "We've never been close. I know that he never really cared about me;

he just found me convenient to use as a hostess occasionally. I don't mind that he doesn't approve. I do feel bad about his children, though. They are so much kinder and more loving than he ever was. I hope that I won't always be estranged from them. I would miss them."

"You know I'd do whatever I could to get along with William," Julian offered, "short of giving you up, that is."

Mavis smiled. "I think the only thing that you can do now is wait. He'll get over it in time."

"By the time he wants something from you, I suppose," he said.

Julian was silent for a few minutes, and Mavis wondered about his debts. That was why he had left, but, so far, he had said nothing about them. She hoped his silence was a good sign.

"How did your business go?" she finally asked.

Julian stood up. "We're going to have to talk about it."

He looked so serious that Mavis became worried. Hadn't he been able to settle his affairs? Maybe they proved to be much larger that he had thought, and he would need to find an heiress. Or maybe he had found an heiress since he had left here. Mavis tried to remind herself that he had only been gone two days, but all her old fears seemed to come back so easily. Julian must have seen her worries, because he came over quickly to where she was.

"You mustn't look so worried," he scolded her.

"A new possibility has opened up and I wanted to talk it over with you."

"Is it an heiress?" she whispered.

"No," he laughed, hugging her tightly, "it's a school."

"A school?" Mavis asked. She had never heard of a school that paid one's debts for them.

"Do you know about some of the boys' schools that Mr. Winfield tries to help?" Mavis nodded. "Well, after I left here on Tuesday, I decided to talk things over with him. I didn't know him very well and have always considered him to be an eccentric, but I have learned that he has sound business sense. When he heard my predicament, he made me an offer. He agreed to settle my debts for me if I would become the headmaster of one of his schools near London."

"What do you know about being a headmaster?" she asked.

"Nothing," Julian admitted. "But that was all right with him. This school has some especially fine teachers, and they are hoping to attract a wealthier class of students there. What I have to offer are my acquaintances. Mr. Winfield hopes that I might be able to influence some of my friends to send their sons to this school."

"It sounds too good to be true," Mavis told him.

"Well, there are drawbacks," he warned.

"Aren't headmasters allowed to be married?" she asked.

"Yes, that's allowed," he laughed. "But there are some other things that you must consider. I can still sell some of my properties to pay off the debts. We don't have to accept this offer."

"It seems perfect to me, but you'd better tell me what these drawbacks are."

"Well, we would have to live at the school. There is a small house there that we could use, but it would be on the school grounds, not private the way this house is." He looked around at the gardens.

"You mean I might not have so many flowers to pick?" she asked. "You'd better not be away very often then."

"You must be serious about this," he told her. "If this is the kind of home that you want, then the school is not the place for us." She nodded and put on a more serious face, which only made Julian laugh.

After he kissed her, he continued. "I'm not sure what my friends would think of my becoming a schoolmaster, but I'm certain that we would not be invited to many exclusive parties. The local gentry would be delighted to include us, but we couldn't spend the season in London."

"School is in session then, anyway, so it seems like you would be neglecting your job to do so," she pointed out.

"I'd be making a fairly small salary," he told her. "There will still be my income from my estate, but the two combined would not allow a very extravagant life."

"I don't think I know how to be extravagant," she reminded him.

"I'm not sure that you are listening to this," he complained. "These things do make a difference, you know."

"Not to me, they don't," she told him gently. "I love you and I don't mind where we live. I have had a few seasons in London, but they have never made me as happy as I have been these past two weeks, since we have met. I suppose I could pass myself off credibly if we were to live the fashionable life, but I don't find it necessary to my happiness. You are the only thing I have to have. You must choose the kind of life that you will be most happy with." She paused. "But remember, I expect to be included in it."

He got up and walked around the small clearing as if he were trying to gather his thoughts together. "I like the idea of the job at the school," he admitted.

"Won't you miss your parties and your fine horses?" she asked him.

"I might," he answered, trying to be honest. "But I'll have you, and I think our life together will be so full that I won't need such things to distract me from boredom."

He came over and pulled her to her feet. "Well, are you willing to become the wife of a lowly headmaster?" he asked.

"Yes," she answered, "as long as you are the lowly headmaster."

He pulled her comfortably against him. "When shall we get married? The new term has already started, and they want me to go down there as soon as possible." He smiled down at her. "Do you happen to have the money for a special license?"

"No," she said sadly. "I fear they're terribly expensive."

"I don't either, but if we post the banns immediately, we won't have to wait very long. Will your brother let you stay here for a few more weeks?"

"He hasn't thrown me out yet."

"He may when he learns of our latest plans."

Hand in hand, they returned to the shade of the taller bushes and trees to discuss their future and the things they would need for their new home.

By late afternoon, Robin was quite tired of the creek, the wall, and William Tolbert. He didn't even stay until dark this time. He felt sure that if Kitty wanted to see him she would have come down here to see if he was waiting. The fact that she was avoiding the area could only mean one thing to him—she did not want to see him.

He rode back to the inn, racking his brain for some other way of talking to Kitty. He was determined to try a new method tomorrow. He could sit on that wall for the rest of his life and still not get a chance to talk to Kitty.

At the same time that Robin was riding back to the inn, Kitty was staring at her ceiling again. She was getting so bored that she was considering apologizing to her father so she could at least get out of the house. She had finished her book and was thinking of playing the pianoforte downstairs, which showed how desperate she was getting.

She wondered where Robin was now. It seemed funny that only a few days ago she had dreaded meeting Lord Scotney, but now she was wishing he would come to see her again. He might be back in London now or at Scotney Park. He might have already married his true love if he had a special license.

When Nellie came to find her before dinner, Kitty poured out the whole story to her. As she had expected, Nellie found it highly romantic.

"It's just like a novel," she sighed when Kitty had finished. "Only better, because it really happened."

Kitty did not show much desire to go into detail about her various meetings with Lord Scotney, but Nellie continued to press her until she was satisfied that Kitty had left nothing out.

"Oh, I bet nothing romantic like that will ever happen to me," Nellie pouted.

"I wish it hadn't happened to me," Kitty said curtly. "I wish somebody had warned me about caring about strangers who don't give a person their right names."

Nellie jumped up. "That's what we can do," she cried. "We can write a novel." Kitty did not look too thrilled with the idea. "It can be based on your tragic love for Robin, only we'll change it a little, so no one will recognize it."

Kitty didn't know who would recognize it anyway, but she didn't tell this to Nellie. She feared that any comment might commit her to Nellie's scheme.

A bell sounded from downstairs.

"After dinner," Nellie promised Kitty. "We'll get started on it right after we eat." Without waiting for an answer, Nellie ran out of the room to finish dressing for dinner.

Kitty arrived downstairs to find that her father was sulking. It seems that he had come home to find Sir Julian in the garden with Mavis, and she had told them that they were going to be married. William was so furious that he had been proven wrong that he was angry at everybody. After dinner, he stomped into the library, closing the door quite firmly behind him.

Mavis went off to make some lists, which she had been doing ever since Julian left. Alicia had received some things from London, and she ran off to her room to study them, leaving the two other girls all alone.

Since Nellie had left her room before dinner, Kitty had been giving her idea some thought. The more she tossed it about in her mind, the more the idea appealed to her. When the girls were left alone after dinner, Nellie was anxious to get started immediately.

"I thought we could change the story at the end, if you want, and have you marry somebody else," Nellie suggested.

"Oh, no," Kitty cried, who had pictured a more romantic future for herself. "If I can't marry Robin, I'm never going to marry anyone."

Nellie was quite pleased with Kitty's idea and began to look for some paper that they could use.

"You have to pretend that you are the heroine and that Robin is the hero," Nellie said. "Then it will get tragic."

Kitty sat down to write while Nellie paced the room.

"Have you thought of a different story, or do you want it to be about you and Robin?" Nellie asked.

"Well, I thought it would be similar to what happened to me, but different in some ways. The girl won't be bound up by restrictions as I am. I thought she could run away to join her true love. They would be happy together, even though they have no money." Kitty told Nellie, "I've decided that being poor is more romantic than being rich."

"Oh, yes," said Nellie. "There are so many more opportunities for sacrifice."

Kitty began to write as Nellie walked around the room dictating her ideas. Their story seemed to move along quite rapidly, through many tragedies, until the sorely tried lovers found happiness together in the end.

"I think that's a really good story," Nellie said as she sank onto Kitty's bed. "It's at least as good as some of the books we get from the circulating library."

"Yes, it might be as good," Kitty said, "but it's

not nearly as long." She held up a very thin stack of papers. "It's only twelve pages long."

"You don't think that's long enough?" Nellie asked. "Maybe it would look longer once it's printed."

"No, I'm sure that it would look shorter, if anything," Kitty said sadly. "Most books are a lot longer than this. We'll have to add something to it."

Nellie thought for a moment. Her natural optimism overcame her disappointment that their novel was not long enough.

"We must have more tragedies," Nellie decided. "The heroine must suffer more to prove her love. Why, she's hardly had to endure anything in what we've already written."

Because the poor heroine had already been almost forced to marry a very wicked old man, was kidnapped, held up by highwaymen, and had to get a job as a housemaid, Kitty thought she had endured quite a bit.

"No," Nellie was firm. "We have to put in more of what she is willing to suffer for her love. All that's happened to her so far was in trying to escape from her evil father." She handed Kitty some more paper and began to pace again. Obviously she felt that pacing was necessary when writing novels.

"What is she willing to endure because of her love?" Nellie asked herself. Because neither girl had much experience with that sort of thing, they had to rely on the novels they had read in the past. "She can't live without him," Nellie began. "Life is meaningless alone."

Kitty was busy writing down what her sister was saying as Nellie began to expand her ideas. At one point, Kitty put her pen down.

"I don't think I could sell my body in the streets of London," she protested. "Not even for Robin."

"This doesn't all have to be true," Nellie told her scornfully. "A writer may stretch the truth a bit, you know. It adds to the dramatic flavor of the story."

Kitty still wasn't sure, but she went back to her writing, as Nellie had returned to her pacing. They worked a little longer, filling several more pages with tragic experiences that should help their story along. They finally stopped when they were both yawning more than they were speaking. Agreeing to continue the next day, both girls went off to bed.

CHAPTER THIRTEEN

Robin was in no hurry to leave the inn the next morning. He was determined not to spend another day waiting by that creek, but he had not come up with any sure way that he might see Kitty. The only alternative that he did think of was to watch the roads into town. Sooner or later, Mr. Tolbert would come in to do some business, and when Robin saw him, he would leave immediately for Crofton Grange. With William out of the way, he might get in to see Kitty.

He spent a long morning strolling through the town. He ate lunch at the inn and then found a shady spot in the courtyard. He settled back to watch the road. About the middle of the afternoon, he was surprised to see a familiar curricle pull into the yard of the inn.

"Trilby, you fiend!" he yelled as his friend climbed down. "I don't want to see you again."

"Didn't she come?" Trilby asked, taking Robin's insults for a normal greeting. "I was sure it would do the trick."

"It did," Robin told him glumly. "What are you doing here, anyway?"

"The question is, what are you still doing here? I thought you'd be long gone. When I saw the paper this morning, I thought you'd be out celebrating. I came down here to help you, though I sure didn't expect to find you still hanging about here. Figured you'd be at the park, since you weren't back in town."

"What are you talking about?" Robin asked. "What was in the paper?"

"You mean you don't know?" Trilby was amazed. He started to laugh. "Julian did the trick!" he told Robin. "The engagement was in the papers. Your

Miss Tolbert and Sir Julian Merriot. Thought you'd be shouting it to the world." Trilby looked puzzled. Robin was not responding the way he had expected. In fact, he seemed to be getting very little response from him at all.

"Robin?" Trilby asked, but his friend did not answer. He was lost in his own thoughts.

Robin was stunned. It was only a few days since he had been making plans with Kitty. How could she be making plans with Julian now? But then, it might not have been her idea. If her father had arranged one marriage, he could always arrange another. Yet Kitty made no attempt to see him. Maybe she was satisfied.

"Didn't take long, did it?" Robin asked bitterly. "Get rid of one and grab another. Money certainly works wonders."

"Hey, don't be so glum," Trilby told him. "You're out of it. Let's celebrate. It's Julian who's got the problems now."

But those are the problems that I wanted, Robin thought. Julian's too old for her, and he doesn't love her like I do.

"What are you staying around for, anyway?" Trilby asked. "You going to be best man at the wedding?"

Robin shook his head in horror. "No, I've had enough of this place. Might as well go." He and Trilby went into the inn and up to Robin's room to collect his bags.

As they were coming down the stairs, the front

door burst open. William Tolbert came charging at Robin.

"So you're still here, are you?" he snarled at Robin. "Thought you'd be long gone by now."

He looked behind Robin but saw only Trilby there. "Where is she?" he threatened. "You'd better tell me where she is right now."

Trilby was not acquainted with Robin's friend, but they were attracting a large crowd in the hallway. He put on his most authoritative face and suggested that they move into a private parlor. The innkeeper looked relieved and opened a door farther down the way. William subsided long enough to enter. The moment the doors were closed, he turned to Robin again.

"Don't try to deny it!" he screamed. "Just tell me where she is."

"Where who is?" Robin finally got a chance to ask.

"Who do you think? Kitty! . . . Who else? . . . What have you done with her?"

"Kitty's gone?" Robin was alarmed. "Where'd she go?" he asked, not realizing that that was what William had been asking him. "But why come here looking for her? Ask Merriot where she is. It didn't take her long to find a replacement for me."

William looked at him strangely. "Merriot's marrying Mavis, not Kitty."

Robin was so relieved when he heard that that he practically hugged William, but he quickly remembered the problem at hand.

"How would I know where she is?" he asked.

"Don't play so innocent," William said. "It's all down here. In her own writing. How she's going to you." William held up a piece of paper he had pulled from his coat. "It's disgusting," he said. He walked over to the window, where the light was better. He looked down at the paper. "Says she can't live without you. She doesn't care what wretched squalor you live in. She's leaving her home and family for you, and"—he paused to glare accusingly at Robin—"says she'll sell her body in the streets of London to buy food for you and the children."

Robin was alarmed that Kitty was gone, but he wasn't sure that he agreed with William's interpretation of the letter he held. It sounded a little too dramatic, considering their relationship. He grabbed it from William's hand.

"You've ruined her," William said. "You bring her back here and marry her, you hear?"

Robin looked at him. The denial he had been about to make was forgotten.

"You can't weasel out of it. You're going to marry her," William insisted.

"Yes," Robin assured him. "I will."

William looked relieved. His main concern was that Kitty had been ruined and that he'd never be able to marry her off. But if Robin would marry her, he wouldn't have to worry. "You bring her back here so it'll look all right," he said, more reasonably. "Just bring her home, and we can keep all of this from getting out. You can be married real soon, and nobody will have to know the truth."

Robin nodded. He was trying to think the whole thing through. He was fairly sure that this note was not written as William thought. It had no signature, nor was it addressed to anyone. It was merely a collection of phrases. He had never seen Kitty's writing, but he assumed she could compose a decent letter.

"How long has she been gone?" he asked William.

He looked embarrassed. "Since early this morning."

"Early this morning! Why did it take you so long to notice she was gone?"

That was a very long time for her to be missing. Robin was feeling more than a little alarmed.

"She was supposed to stay in the house," William tried to explain. "I wasn't letting her out because of a disagreement we'd had. I thought she was in her room. Seems that she slipped out this morning. Her horse is gone, too."

Robin felt they had better start looking for her immediately. She had already been missing for six hours. There was no telling what mischief she'd get into in that time. He called a groom and had his horse brought out front, while he told William to go back to his home. Robin would check there later in case she had come home by herself. Trilby offered to help, but not knowing Kitty, there was little he could do. William left, and Trilby walked out with Robin.

"There was a lot back there that I didn't understand, but I did get the impression that you aren't against marrying this girl. Is that right?"

Robin nodded as he waited anxiously for his horse.

"Didn't Daisy get the engagement broken?" he asked, thoroughly puzzled.

"She certainly did," Robin told him. If he could just find Kitty and she was all right, everything was going to work out after all.

"Why are you letting yourself get put back on the hook, then?" Trilby wanted to know.

"Because I love her," Robin said simply. His horse was ready and he mounted quickly. "I'll see you later."

Still very confused, Trilby watched him ride off. And just who was it that Julian was going to marry?

Robin didn't think that the note was intended as a farewell letter, but Kitty had done some pretty strange things, so he couldn't be sure. At least he knew why she had not come to the creek to look for him. But suppose she had decided to run away; where would she have gone? He liked to think that she would look for him, but he had no reason to believe that she would. Supposing she was looking for me, Robin wondered, where would she go? He had been in town all day and she had not come to the inn; not that he had noticed anyway. He doubted that she knew where he lived in London; besides, he couldn't see her traveling all that distance by herself. That only left Scotney Park, which was only a few hours away. Assuming that

William had searched his own grounds, Robin turned his horse in the direction of his estate. He would pass along Crofton Grange for a while, and he would keep his eyes open for any sign of her.

He traveled along for quite a while, meeting no one and seeing no sign of Kitty. As he passed by the creek, he slowed his horse down. He wondered, if he had gone there today, would he have met Kitty as she rode away?

Just as he was moving his horse back to the middle of the road, he caught a movement behind some trees. He rode across the grass and saw a horse grazing a few feet away. It was saddled, yet it seemed to be roaming freely. As he started to move closer to it, he heard a voice calling, down close to the stream. Maybe it was his imagination, but it sounded like Kitty.

He quickly rode toward the sound and came up to the wall. There, amid the bushes, right next to the wall, sat Kitty. She looked a little dirty, but unhurt.

"What are you doing here?" he asked impatiently.

Kitty had been quite glad to see Robin approach, but she did not care much for his greeting. "I'm just resting," she said obstinately.

Robin dismounted and walked over to where she sat. There were a few branches in her hair, but not enough to hold her here for six hours. It was then that he noticed that her position was very awkward.

"What happened?" he asked in alarm. "Are you

hurt?" He pulled some of the branches away so he could get closer to her.

"No, I'm fine," she reassured him. She was feeling more kindly toward him now that he had shown some concern. "Guess what, Robin! I jumped the wall!"

He didn't seem to share her excitement. "Then why are you on the ground?" he asked.

"Well, I still fell off, but I stayed on until after Dancer jumped." She was very excited about her accomplishment, even if Robin didn't see it as a great achievement. "It was when I fell that I got my foot caught here." She lifted her skirt slightly, and he could see her foot wedged tightly into a broken space in the wall.

"How did you manage to do that?" he asked rudely. He was relieved to find her well but was getting irritated by her lack of contrition.

"Well, I didn't do it on purpose." She could be just as rude as he could. "And nobody asked you to stay to help me. So if you're too busy to spare the time, you can go." She turned away to inspect her foot. When she looked up again, Robin was nowhere in sight. She forgot that she had dismissed him and began to call frantically.

"Robin!" she screamed. "Robin, please come back."

"I only went to get my knife," he said, returning from the other side of the wall, "and I tied my horse so he wouldn't stray."

"Oh," she said, embarrassed that she had shown panic so easily.

He examined the wall closely. "It's going to take a while because the only tool I've got is my knife. Are you sure your foot doesn't hurt you?"

"Only when I try to loosen it," she said. "I can move my toes without pain; I just can't get it out." She tried to pull it out again; something she must have tried many times already, Robin thought. But she was not in the proper position to free it. She soon stopped trying and blinked back the tears that came to her eyes.

"Maybe I should go get help," Robin suggested.

"Oh, no," she pleaded. "Please don't leave me again. I'm sure you can do it." She didn't want to admit it to Robin, but she had been frightened by herself. And the fear that she had just felt a few minutes ago convinced her that she didn't want to be left alone again.

"I'll try," Robin promised. "Maybe I can work some of these stones free." He was not too confident, but he could see that Kitty was afraid to be left alone there. He began to chip away at the mortar holding the stones in place.

"I hope you aren't going to do this kind of thing often once we're married," he teased.

"But . . . we aren't getting married," Kitty said. "Father said it was off."

"Well, he's decided that it's on again," Robin told her as he worked. "He thinks that you ran off with me and demands that I marry you to save your reputation."

"Oh, no." Kitty was quite distressed. Robin

stopped and looked up at her. "I'm so sorry, Robin. I never meant to involve you in all this. After all the trouble we've both had trying to break the contract. I'll talk to Father, I promise I will, and get you free of me again. Don't worry."

"Just what trouble have you gone to to break the contract?" he asked.

"Oh, you know," she said. "All those stories. Nellie's was the best, I have to admit."

Robin put down his knife. "Do you mean that all that wasn't true?" he asked, getting angry. "She made up all that about Edward?"

Kitty nodded nervously. She hoped he wasn't going to get mad about it. After all, what difference did it make now?

"Just what was the purpose of those stories, to see how much nonsense I might believe?"

"No," Kitty cried. "We did it for you. You told me about the woman you loved and we—Nellie and I—thought that if you were released from the contract you could marry her." She began to feel a little uncertain under his angry glare. "We were just trying to save you some trouble."

"Trying to save me trouble!" he exclaimed. "What trouble?"

"Well, if Father had let you out of the contract then, you would not have had to hire that woman to say she was your wife. I admit that that was effective, but it was kind of a shock at first. You might not have liked our interfering, but you have to admit, our way was more polite." She didn't know why he was so upset about it. They had meant well.

"Sure," he said, and went back to work.

"Why are you still around here anyway?" she asked. "I thought you'd have been gone long ago."

"I've been spending my days sitting on this wall, hoping you'd come by."

"Why?" Kitty asked. "Oh," she continued, thinking she knew the reason, "you didn't have to apologize about that woman. I understood. Really I did. I was a bit stunned at first, because I just couldn't believe that you had married that woman. . . . Not after you had been making plans with me. . . . I did think she might be your mistress, though. When Father came back from town and told me you'd hired her, I knew right away why you'd done it. It was the only way that he'd let you go. Father was very angry, but I told him it was all his own fault for refusing to listen to us when we told him we weren't suited." She stopped and watched Robin take a handkerchief out of his pocket. He folded it diagonally and then into a narrow strip. "What are you going to do with that?" she asked.

"I am going to gag you," he said calmly. "I think that it's the only way I'm going to get a chance to say something."

"Well, I was only trying to let you know I understood." She hastily retreated in silence as he brought the cloth near her.

"Every time I try to talk to you, you start explaining things and tell me how you understand, and I never get a chance. You are going to listen now and not run off until I've finished. Understand that?"

She nodded but couldn't resist adding, "I can't very well leave until you get my foot loose."

He kept the handkerchief in his hand in case he needed it. "I did not hire that woman, first of all. A friend of mine did. He thought it was a terrific plan to get me out of the engagement. You see, I had asked him for help before I had ever met you. It never occurred to me to tell him that I'd changed my mind." She seemed to be quiet, so he went back to loosening the stones. "It came as a complete surprise to me when she arrived. I paid her because Trilby had promised that I would. Even though I had not wanted her help, I felt I had to at least pay her expenses down here and back. Unfortunately, your father came as I was paying her and deliberately misunderstood everything. I was waiting around here to explain it to you, but you never came."

"Father wouldn't let me out of the house," she explained.

"So he told me today." Robin got one stone loose. If he could remove the other one, she should be able to get her foot out. He worked at it, while Kitty thoughtfully watched him. After a few minutes, the stone came free.

He gingerly moved her foot, which was rather swollen from her attempts to get it free, until he could ease it out of the hole. He helped her away from the bushes, over to the wall. She tried to stand alone but found that her legs couldn't support her. She could have leaned against the wall, but Robin's arms were there helping her before she knew it.

"Your legs are probably just stiff from sitting there so long," he reassured her. "You'll be all right in a few minutes. Then we'd better get you home. Your father was very worried about you. I don't like to keep him in suspense."

Mention of her father reminded Kitty that he was trying to force Robin to marry her again. "I'll talk to him as soon as I get back," Kitty told him. "If I can manage my horse, you could just go. I'll tell him you had nothing to do with it. If you're not around anymore, he'll have to accept what I say."

Robin pushed her slightly away from him, so he could look down into her face. "Would you please stop trying to manage things for me? I am not trying to get out of marrying you. I haven't since I met you. You are the only one who is determined that we shouldn't marry."

"What about that other woman?" she reminded him. "The one you said you loved. . . . You did say it, didn't you?"

He looked down at her with a rather alarming smile. "Yes," he told her. "I can't deny that I said it."

Kitty had been sincerely hoping that he would, and looked very disappointed. But Robin only laughed.

"I fell in love with a grubby little girl who falls into bushes, steps in the mud, and meddles in things she doesn't understand." He tilted Kitty's head back. "And every time I try to tell her, she comes up with some totally outrageous story to distract me." He bent down and kissed her. After a rather long interval, which cleared any doubts that might have lingered in Kitty's mind about who this "other woman" was, he lifted his head. "If she does anything else to get our wedding called off, I am going to abduct her."

"Oh, Robin," she said breathlessly. "I didn't really want the wedding to be cancelled. I was just trying to help you."

"Well, don't help me like that anymore," he warned her. He looked down at her smiling face resting against his coat. "You're sure you don't mind marrying me?" he asked.

"Oh, no," she said. "I wanted to all along. That's what was so hard. I was trying to help you, but I only succeeded in making myself miserable and lonely. Nellie kept telling me it was romantic, but I didn't really want you to marry somebody else."

"Why not?" he teased.

She looked up at him shyly. "Because I was sure that I loved you more than that other woman, whoever she was."

He held her tightly and bent down to kiss her again, both of them forgetting that her father was waiting anxiously.